What a har he was!

'Don't you underst
ing with people wh~~o are having t~~o
own *crises*?' he demanded. 'And the question of
fertility yields its own particular problems because
it is something so intensely *personal*. Every
couple assume, rightly or wrongly, that they will
be able to bring their own children into the world.
That is, after all, the point of marriage. . .'

Maisy's eyes widened, her misery forgotten. 'And
what about love?' she questioned indignantly
before she stopped to think. 'I thought that was
what marriage was about.'

Matthew's laugh was odd—a mixture of cynicism
and resignation. 'Only for dreamers, Dr Jackson,'
he answered damningly. 'Only for dreamers.'

Sharon Kendrick had a variety of jobs before training as a nurse and a medical secretary, and found that she enjoyed working in a caring environment. She was encouraged to write by her doctor husband after the birth of their two children and much of her medical information comes from him and from friends. She lives in Surrey where her husband is a GP. She has previously written medical romances as Sharon Wirdnam and now, as Sharon Kendrick, divides her time between the medical romances and Mills & Boon Presents.

WAIT AND SEE

BY
SHARON KENDRICK

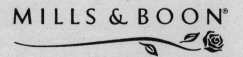
MILLS & BOON®

To Jenny and Geoff Wightwick
and their adorable children
Lucy, Tom and Alice

All the characters in this book have no existence outside the imagination of the author, and have no relation whatsoever to anyone bearing the same name or names. They are not even distantly inspired by any individual known or unknown to the author, and all the incidents are pure invention.

*First published in Great Britain 1997
Harlequin Mills & Boon Limited,
Eton House, 18-24 Paradise Road, Richmond, Surrey TW9 1SR*

© Sharon Kendrick 1997

ISBN 0 263 80439 9

*Set in Times 11 on 12½ pt. by
Rowland Phototypesetting Limited
Bury St Edmunds, Suffolk*

03-9711-43769-D

*Printed and bound in Great Britain
by Mackays of Chatham PLC, Chatham*

CHAPTER ONE

'WHAT do you mean, you won't *be* there?'

Still reeling from the bombshell that her sister had just dropped, Maisy Jackson pushed a wave of wheaten hair off her forehead and stared down with disbelief at the telephone she was holding. 'But, Sarah, why?'

'Because Jamie's been given the opportunity to do a job swap with an Australian consultant,' explained her sister patiently, 'and we're going to Sydney for six months.'

Maisy gulped. 'Six *months*?'

'Yep! And I can't wait! Maisy, it's the chance of a lifetime—surely you can see that?'

'And what about Harriet? What about her schooling?' With a neatly filed, unvarnished fingernail Maisy rubbed at a spot of ink which marred the pristine whiteness of her shirt cuff. And it was a brand-new shirt, too! 'Surely uprooting her to the other side of the world will disrupt all that?'

She heard her sister's voice soften instinctively as she began to speak about her stepdaughter.

'Not really, no. I don't think it will. Harriet is really looking forward to it and her teacher says that any disruption will be far outweighed by the advantages of living in a different country for six months. And children are tremendously adaptable.'

Maisy frowned; she couldn't help it. She wanted to be pleased at her sister's news, but it was all so *sudden*!

Maisy was still feeling vulnerable after her broken engagement. She had been looking forward to lots of cosy chats and outings with her newly married baby sister.

Not that she had been planning to monopolise her totally—far from it! She had planned to offer to babysit for Sarah and Jamie any time they wanted to go out, and this would have been no hardship since she absolutely adored her niece.

And this bombshell Sarah had just dropped did not fit in with her plans. Not at all.

'But that was the main reason I applied for the research job at Southbury Hospital in the first place,' she grumbled. 'Because my brother-in-law was an obstetrician there—'

'No, you didn't!' contradicted her sister. 'You applied because Southbury Hospital has the biggest and best infertility clinic outside London.'

'Well, I did like the fact that you and I might get the chance to see a bit more of each other,' said Maisy truthfully. 'With you working as a midwife and all.'

There was a funny gulping sound from Sarah at the other end of the phone. 'But I'm not.'

'Not what?'

'Not working as a midwife. Or, rather, I won't be. Not in Australia, anyway, or for some time to come. Perhaps never again.'

'What *are* you wittering on about, Sarah?'

There was a pause. Then it all came out in one excited, breathless rush, in the same voice Maisy remembered her using as a child when she'd seen the piles of Christmas presents stacked beneath the tree. 'Maisy. . . Maisy. . . I'm. . .*pregnant*!'

Taken completely by surprise, Maisy was shocked by the sudden twisting lurch of envy in her stomach and wondered what had caused it. A *baby*? She surely wasn't jealous of the fact that her sister was having a baby? That was the last thing she herself wanted. Wasn't it?

'How pregnant?' she swallowed.

Sarah's voice was bashful. 'Well, only five and a half weeks—'

'Sarah, that's hardly—'

'Yes, I *know* you're not really supposed to say anything for at least three months—until the pregnancy is properly established—but, oh, Maisy, I'm so excited that I felt I'd *burst* if I didn't tell someone soon!' Suddenly she sounded terribly insecure. 'You *are* pleased for me, aren't you, Maisy?'

Feeling ashamed of her somewhat lukewarm response to the news, Maisy forced herself to sound enthusiastic. 'Of course I'm pleased, you ninny!' But inside she was still reeling with the shock of her sister's news.

How on earth could Sarah, who was the baby of the family, be having a baby herself? But, there again, Sarah had a very loving relationship with her stepdaughter, Harriet, who was nearly eleven, so was it really surprising that she now felt mature enough to have a baby of her own? 'It's just a little *sudden*, that's all,' she said slowly, then couldn't resist asking, 'Was it planned?'

Sarah giggled. 'Well, not exactly, no! It's just that Jamie and I went away for the weekend, and he completely forgot to—'

'That's *enough*!' said Maisy disapprovingly. 'A simple yes or no would have sufficed. I really don't want to hear intimate details about your sex life, thank you very much!'

On the other end of the phone Sarah sighed. 'Honestly, Maisy, you're such a prude! Heaven only knows how you manage as an obstetric and gynaecological registrar, having to quiz people about their sex lives all day!'

'I am *not* a prude.' Maisy defended herself instantly but her cheeks went pink because sister's joke had unintentionally hit on a very touchy subject. 'I just don't particularly want to hear intimate details about what you and Jamie get up to in bed—'

'But we weren't actually *in* bed at the time!' Sarah giggled again. 'We—'

'That's enough!' Maisy snapped. To her amazement and fury, she found herself flushing even pinker and was grateful for the fact that her sister was unable to see her because she would have teased her mercilessly. And then her bleeper began to shrill loudly and she felt an overwhelming sense of relief. 'Sarah, that's my bleeper. I have to go. Listen, I'll see you next week at Southbury—'

'But that's the whole point. . .you won't. We're off at the weekend.'

'This weekend? But surely you can't be going to

Australia *that* soon? I mean, you've only just told me—'

'We've been arranging it for months but we kept it very quiet. We didn't want to say anything in case it didn't happen. We were worried that people might try and talk us out of it. And it would have raised Harriet's hopes too much if it had all fallen through. But now we've told her, and she's over the moon! And the guy that Jamie is swapping with wanted it to happen as soon as possible. He's more keen than we are, if that's possible.'

'I see,' said Maisy, suddenly feeling very flat indeed. 'So who's Jamie's Australian replacement, then?'

'*Oh*!' Sarah sounded smug. 'That's the *other* big bit of news! His name is Matthew Gallagher and he's—'

Maisy's eyebrows disappeared beneath her thick, wavy fringe. 'Yes. I've heard of him,' she said with dry understatement. Matthew Gallagher? Coming to Southbury Hospital? Maisy was impressed, despite her determination not to be. 'He's one of the world's leading authorities on infertility—'

'He's also *ve-ry* hunky!' said Sarah mischievously. 'He's been here for two weeks so that Jamie can show him the ropes and, believe *me*, Maisy, the man is sex on legs—'

'*Sar-ah*!'

'So if you happen to be looking for a replacement for Giles then you need look no further! Thank heavens you dumped that creep! I knew the very first time I met him that he was the most boring—'

'Sarah, I have to answer my bleeper,' cut in Maisy hastily, not wishing to hear yet *another* member of her family banging on about how much they had disliked Giles. 'If you thought he was *that* bad why didn't you say something at the time?' she demanded frostily.

'Because you would never have listened!' came her sister's cheerful response. 'You never do!'

Maisy smiled. 'And will I see you before you go?'

'Yes—if you can manage to get home this weekend,' said Sarah. 'Can you? We're taking Harriet to say goodbye to Mum and Dad, and Benedict and Verity are going to be there with the children. Do try and come, Maisy—we'd love to see you.'

'I'll try,' said Maisy, trying to sound as chirpy as possible but unsure whether she sounded convincing. Because it was all too easy to anticipate what the weekend would actually be like. Everyone, even her parents, all lovey-dovey and cooing sweet nothings at each other and their children.

Whilst she stood on the sidelines and watched, unattached and unemotional.

Or as Giles had so sweetly put it, 'You're nothing but a frigid little bitch, Maisy.'

As she punched out the number of the hospital switchboard Maisy caught a glimpse of her sooty-grey eyes in the mirror. Was he right?

Her over-generous mouth turned down at the corners defiantly. And, even if he *was* right, who cared?

Men!

They were more trouble than they were worth!

'Dr Jackson,' she said crisply into the receiver. 'You're bleeping me.'

'Can you ring Labour Ward?' said the operator. 'Urgently.'

'Right,' said Maisy, thinking that she might as well go down there before she started her afternoon gynae list in Theatre.

She stifled a huge yawn as she set off along one of the ancient, echoing corridors. She had been on call last night with a long and tricky delivery of twins which had kept her awake for most of it. This recent stint at Birmingham's busy city centre hospital had been the hardest job of her life so far. She couldn't remember the last time she had had an unbroken night when she had been on duty, and her weekends and nights off had been spent mainly catching up on sleep.

And returning wedding presents.

Maybe Sarah and Jamie *wouldn't* be at Southbury Hospital as a sort of family welcoming committee but at least a year doing research might give her a bit of a well-earned rest.

A year by the sea, doing a job which had blissfully regular hours, with the added bonus of weekends off. An opportunity to take stock of her life and decide what she wanted to do with the rest of it now that she was no longer going to marry Giles.

It sounded like bliss.

And who knew what could happen? She might even be able to start living like a normal twenty-seven-year-old instead of an emotional mess.

Maisy couldn't wait!

CHAPTER TWO

FOR a doctor who was often up all night an eight o'clock start seemed almost like a lie-in. More importantly, the threat of sleeping late was almost negligible.

Well, that had been Maisy's theory, and Maisy had always *tried* to be a punctual person.

Unfortunately, the reality was that on a bright summer's morning when she *should* have been donning her white coat and heading off for her first day at the Southbury assisted conception clinic she was, in fact, gazing in stupefied horror at the alarm clock by her bed, which read five minutes to nine precisely.

'It can't be!' she exclaimed aloud, as if half expecting the clock to talk back to her.

Oh, *why* had she stayed on for Sunday lunch after Sarah's and Jamie's farewell party? A Sunday lunch, which had stretched on to late afternoon champagne followed by a swim in her parents' swimming pool. It had been tremendous fun at the time, and it had taken very little persuasion from the united Jackson clan to get Maisy to live dangerously—a trait she had all but stifled under her ex-fiancé's instructions—but look how she was paying for it now!

This was not how she had planned her first morning as a researcher in one of the most prestigious units in the country, she thought as she scrambled out of the narrow bed which seemed to be standard issue in all doctors' rooms.

She should have been about to eat a sensible breakfast to set her up for the day ahead, instead of grabbing a dry biscuit on the run. And she *should* have been grinning with satisfaction at her reflection in the mirror right now, instead of grimacing at the sight of her unmade-up face and her unwashed hair.

Oh, *heck*, she thought, with one final, despairing look. Even for a person who was so hit-and-miss about her appearance, she couldn't remember ever having looked quite so grim.

Wheat-coloured hair was all very well in its way, but it *did* tend to go hand in hand with the kind of freckle-spattered and milky-pale skin which made you look positively anaemic unless you were a expert at applying blusher. Which Maisy most definitely was not.

Not for the first time she cursed a cruel fate which had passed her over in favour of her siblings when handing out the famous green Jackson eyes, with their thick dark lashes which needed no embellishment.

True, she had inherited her grandmother's slate-grey eyes and slim, leggy build, and her pale, wavy hair was as thick as honey, but hers were the kind of looks which needed attention if they were to shine. And shining she wasn't—not this morning, anyway.

She pulled on her white coat and, thrusting a notebook and clutch of pens in the pocket, slammed out of her room in the doctors' mess and headed off towards the clinic.

Even at a run, it took her almost ten minutes to get there, and this was due to the fact that the clinic had been set in the prettiest part of the hospital grounds but at some distance from the doctors' residence.

Maisy supposed that the combination of trees and shrubs, together with the salty tang of the sea air, might make couples more relaxed about what was ultimately a very personal and emotive subject— the ability to procreate.

She hurried through the automatic glass doors and almost collided with a tall, slim nurse.

'Gosh! Sorry!' said Maisy breathlessly. 'I'm afraid I wasn't really looking where I was going—'

'No, you weren't,' came the cool and not particularly friendly retort.

Maisy blinked in surprise, her friendly smile dying on her lips at something in the nurse's body language. She looked at her a bit more closely.

The young woman was obviously a staff nurse, Maisy decided, since she had a large display of different badges glittering on the front of her uniform dress.

And what a uniform! thought Maisy somewhat enviously.

It was the most flattering nurse's dress that Maisy had ever seen, and which made her feel even more of a scarecrow. A navy blue polka-dotted dress, which looked as though it might be made of some kind of voile, with foaming frills of lace adorning the short sleeves which matched the cap perched on top of the woman's glossy dark hair.

But the feminine outfit did not marry very well with the distinctly unwelcoming expression which was currently distorting the staff nurse's pretty face.

Maisy gave an inward sigh as she recognised what was an unpalatable fact of hospital life. That some nurses resented doctors if they happened to be female. That, for *some* reason, they found it difficult to take orders from another woman and regarded female doctors as the enemy. And the good-looking ones were often the worse.

Like this one, for example, thought Maisy, as she registered doe-like brown eyes and magnolia-pale skin. This one was *very* good-looking. She cleared her throat and made an effort to pin the smile back onto her mouth.

'Hello!' she said brightly. 'I'm Maisy Jackson and I'm the new—'

'I know who you are,' responded the nurse, without a glimmer of a smile. 'And you're late. Over an hour late, in fact.'

Maisy was momentarily stunned by the nurse's rudeness until she felt a surge of the famous Jackson fighting spirit. 'I may be late,' she retorted crisply, 'but it isn't really your place to chastise me, is it, Nurse?'

'No,' came a disapproving and laconic drawl from just behind her. 'It's mine.'

It sounded ridiculously fanciful to say that the deep male voice sounded some warning bell in Maisy's heart but that was *exactly* what it felt like.

Maisy felt as though she had been waiting all her life to hear that voice.

She spun round, hoping against hope that the owner of the voice would be short and rotund, possibly with a pair of thick-rimmed spectacles and beads of sweat dewing his upper lip, but she was out of luck for he was none of these things.

Instead, there stood a man whose looks seemed to have been designed to give visual pleasure to all women. Because Maisy couldn't think of a single female of *her* acquaintance who wouldn't be bowled over by the man standing in front of her!

He was tall—well over six feet tall—and, although he wasn't in the least bit muscle-bound, he looked as if he had untold strength in those gloriously long limbs.

His hair was dark, but not the raven-black hair of romantic heroes—it was much more subtle than that. It was what you might even call *brown*, Maisy supposed reluctantly.

She had always thought of brown hair as being boring and unattractive but, then, she had never realised before just how many different and glorious shades of brown there could be in a head of hair. Some strands were golden, others walnut and here and there she could catch a glimpse of mahogany and cinnamon.

His face was angled, full of interesting planes and shadows, with the most beautiful pair of cheekbones Maisy could ever recall seeing. But the eyes were what *really* threw her. They were slanting and green. Not bright emerald-green, like her brother's and sisters' eyes, but an infinitely more subtle mid-sage colour. And the eyes were shaded by thick, dark, dead straight eyelashes, which gave his face an oddly secretive appearance and made Maisy's heart lurch even more.

And right now those eyes were narrowed even more than what Maisy assumed was their habitual slant, and it made him look thoroughly enigmatic.

'You must be Dr Jackson,' he said slowly, in a accent which defied description. 'Dr Maisy Jackson.'

Something in the derisive twist of his mouth made her feel confrontational. But then confrontation seemed her only source of protection from the uncomfortable feelings he was provoking. 'Did you overhear the nurse say my name?' she asked him pertly. 'Or was that pure deduction on your part?'

Irritation sparked from the green eyes.

'Neither,' he said, his perfect lips tightening repressively. 'I am the consultant in charge of the unit. And, consequently, it would be fairly dense of me not to be aware of exactly who is about to join the payroll. Wouldn't it, Dr Jackson?

'Yes,' said Maisy slowly, thinking how very formal he sounded. Unfriendly, too. 'I suppose it would. And you must be Matthew Gallagher.' She surveyed him with unblinking slate-grey eyes.

'Well deduced,' he mocked.

'And you're Australian?' she asked him stupidly, aware that she sounded more like an awestruck teenager at a party than a grown woman who had a very respectable number of letters appearing after her name.

'Well done again,' he answered unhelpfully, his eyes flicking over her with all the impartial scrutiny of a lab technician analysing the contents of a syringe.

Maisy was consumed with the urgent need to fill the sudden, rather awkward silence. 'You don't sound particularly Australian,' she observed, aware but uncaring of the dark, attractive staff nurse at her side sucking in a deep breath of disapproval— presumably for having dared make such a personal remark to the *consultant*!

'No?' His voice deepened into a deep, rough Aussie accent. 'Expected me to say "G'day, sheila!" while wearing a hat with corks dangling from it, did you, Dr Jackson?'

The critical note in his question was unmistakable. 'Not really, no. That would be terribly unimaginative of me, wouldn't you say?' mused Maisy thoughtfully because he spoke with a refined and very cool confidence which she had rarely met before. In his manner of speech he reminded her very much of her brother Benedict's tutor at Cambridge, and nobody could have been more English than *he*! 'Actually, I was thinking less of what you actually said and more about the way you *said* it.'

'Meaning?' came the dangerously soft prompt.

Maisy shrugged, strangely uncomfortable under that penetrating green stare. With that ominous look making his aristocratic features look as if they had been carved from marble, he did not at that moment look like the type of man who would be in the least bit flattered to be compared to a Cambridge scholar. Much too foppish for him—and he would probably think she was casting aspersions on his manhood! 'Oh, you know. . .'

'No, I don't know,' he ground out unhelpfully.

Embarrassed now, she tried to backtrack. 'I just—'

'You just decided to stereotype a whole nation simply on the evidence of a few juvenile television programmes featuring kangaroos and kooka- burras—which you doubtless watched in your youth. Didn't you?'

'I did not. I have never been particularly fond of generalisations.' Maisy stared directly into his eyes, taken aback by the sudden vitriol in his voice. 'Just why are you attacking me, Dr Gallagher?'

Their eyes met in a long antagonistic moment. 'Is that what I'm doing, then?' he quizzed coolly.

'You know you are.' She forced herself to remem- ber that she was a registrar, a well-qualified and well-respected member of the medical profession. 'And I'd like to know why. Surely not just because I overslept?'

He gave a curved smile which was the most humourless she had ever witnessed. 'Not here, Dr Jackson,' he said curtly. 'You'd better come into my consulting room!' And he swiftly turned on his heel.

Talk about feeling chastised! He really had *no* right to speak to her in that way, thought Maisy mutinously.

The dark, glossy nurse beside her sniggered, and for two pins Maisy would have walked straight out of the building and back to her grotty little room in the doctors' mess.

But she couldn't do that. After all, this was real life—not fantasy. This was her job for the next year, maybe more. She needed the experience and she needed the reference that working here would provide. A *good* reference. And if that meant swallowing her pride and forcing herself to humour her new and very sour-faced consultant then so be it.

'*Do* excuse me,' said Maisy with icy civility to the nurse, and then leaned forward to peer at her name badge. 'Nurse. . .Marsh,' she finished. And, with a glower in the staff nurse's direction, she followed Dr Gallagher into his consulting room.

Or, rather, into her absent brother-in-law's consulting room, which Maisy had never seen before.

It was very large room which reflected the status of the doctor who was in charge of the entire unit, and it had vast windows which overlooked the beautifully tended grounds outside. Through a clump of trees Maisy could just catch a glimpse of the sea, and she could hear the lazy and discordant cawing sounds of seagulls in the distance.

As consulting rooms went it was surprising since there were no obvious signs that it belonged to a doctor. No stethoscope or thermometers or health charts adorned the pale walls—just a few exquisitely executed water colours. Nice one, Jamie, thought Maisy fondly.

Only a large wooden desk covered with piles of

papers and notes indicated that it was a place of work, but it could just as easily have belonged to a business executive as to a doctor.

Matthew Gallagher looked up as she walked in. 'Shut the door,' he said curtly.

Maisy felt like asking him if he had forgotten the magic word 'please', but something about the rather forbidding glance which hardened his shuttered features stopped her. She shut the door.

He went behind his desk but remained standing so that, physically, he was looking down at her.

'You asked why I was attacking you,' he said, his face showing not a trace of emotion. 'Which is overstating my attitude just a little. Censure might have been closer to the mark—'

'I really think—'

'Please don't interrupt,' he directed coolly, and Maisy was forced to bite back her instinct response that *he* had interrupted *her*! 'I was critical because I have high standards—both in my professional *and* my personal life.'

'Aren't you just the perfect one?' snapped Maisy, stung.

He didn't react. 'I think it creates a particularly poor impression and puts me in a particularly bad humour if a key member of my staff can't even make the effort to be punctual on her first day.' His eyes glittered. 'Or did you imagine that your brother-in-law's position here would guarantee you some kind of special treatment?'

Maisy froze, unable to believe her ears. 'Would you mind explaining that remark?' she said quietly.

He shrugged impressively broad shoulders beneath the crisply pressed white coat he wore. 'Maybe you thought you'd have an easy ride here since your sister happens to be married to the consultant—'

'I see you really *have* been doing your homework, Dr Gallagher,' said Maisy in a voice of mock admiration and was rewarded with a frown. 'But just how far-reaching is this nepotism supposed to be? Do you think I'm about to swan off for three-hour lunches every day and knock off at five every evening on the dot?'

'You tell me,' he challenged softly.

Maisy met that intense sage stare without flinching. 'OK, I will. I wouldn't *dream* of abusing my position as Jamie Brennan's sister-in-law by adopting sloppy work practices,' she told him icily. 'Even if I tried, Jamie is far too professional to tolerate such unprofessional behaviour from *anyone* in his unit. And, believe me, his standards are so exacting that he will expect me to work *harder* than the average registrar. Not less.'

'I'm very pleased to hear it,' he commented.

'Good.'

Their eyes met for a long moment and Maisy felt a sudden shiver of awareness whisper its way up her spine.

'As it is,' he added waspishly, 'you've missed the opportunity for me to talk you through the unit's timetable and answer any queries or worries you might have before starting work here. People sometimes have ethical and moral concerns about fertility treatments.'

'And with good reason,' agreed Maisy pensively. 'It's an emotive subject whose repercussions should never be taken lightly.'

He looked slightly taken aback at her sudden insightful remark, and knitted his dark brows even further together. 'If you had been here when you should have been,' he put in repressively, 'we might have even got off to a good start over a cup of coffee—'

Maisy could have screamed with frustration. 'But you still haven't given me a chance to explain *why* I was late—'

'Oh, I'm sure you can manufacture *something* masquerading as an explanation, Dr Jackson,' he answered in a voice which was crisp with criticism. 'But I don't consider late nights or hangovers or rapturous mornings in bed with lovers to be an adequate excuse.'

Maisy shuddered as his words brought back the reality of mornings in bed with Giles. And shuddered with guilt, too, because Dr Holier-than-thou Gallagher was right. Because if she hadn't drunk all that unaccustomed champagne at her parents' house yesterday afternoon then she wouldn't have overslept this morning. Nevertheless, everyone was allowed one mistake.

Weren't they?

'You're jumping to some mighty harsh conclusions, aren't you?' she told him. 'I was in bed on my own.'

His eyes narrowed even more at this piece of information. 'Harsh?' He looked surprised at her choice of word. 'I don't think so. Realistic would be a more accurate assessment, given the frantic nature of most junior doctors' love lives. But enlighten me. Why *were* you late, if it wasn't passion?'

'M-my alarm clock didn't go off, if you must know!'

'Weak,' was his only response to that. 'Just don't let it happen again. As it is, because it was your first day we had already given you an extra hour's leeway—'

Maisy wrinkled her nose up in confusion. 'I'm not sure I understand what you mean.'

He glared. 'I am in Theatre, scanning, by seven-thirty in the morning, *every* morning—'

'*Every* morning?' echoed Maisy faintly.

'That's right. Or were you expecting a holiday because this is your research year, Dr Jackson?' he questioned silkily.

This was so close to the truth that Maisy found her cheeks growing a give-away shade of pink.

His smile was mocking and triumphant. 'Well, at least you had the grace not to deny it,' he conceded.

Maisy felt about seven years old. 'Is that all, Dr Gallagher?'

'It is not all. While we're on the subject of atti-tudes to work, you should also know that I am unwilling to tolerate shabby standards of dress.'

His eyes roved over her critically and Maisy became acutely and miserably aware of her unmade-up face and her unwashed hair, her mismatched clothes and her unpolished shoes. And not just because it fell short of her usual professional standards. It hurt her pride, Maisy realised, for a man like Matthew Gallagher to see her looking such a *mess*.

The question she didn't want to ask herself was just *why* it should matter.

'I didn't have time to sort through my wardrobe,' she said miserably, wishing that she could wake up and start the whole morning once again. And not daring to tell him that she had got in so late from her parents' house that her clothes were still firmly wedged into two suitcases in her room!

But the cold glitter from his sage-green eyes indicated that her distress cut no ice with him. What a hard and exacting man he was!

'Don't you understand that every day we are dealing with people who are having to endure their own *crisis*?' he demanded. 'And the question of fertility yields its own particular problems because it is something so intensely *personal*. Every couple assume, rightly or wrongly, that they will be able to bring their own children into the world. That is, after all, the point of marriage. . .'

Maisy's eyes widened, her misery forgotten. How archaic could you get? she wondered. 'And what about love?' she questioned indignantly before she stopped to think about it. 'I thought that was what marriage was about.'

His laugh was odd—a mixture of cynicism and resignation. 'Only for dreamers, Dr Jackson,' he answered damningly. 'Only for dreamers.'

Maisy looked at him intently. Now what, she wondered fleetingly, had happened to make such a spectacularly good-looking man into such a cynic? 'Really?' she queried in disbelief.

He frowned. 'Haven't you looked at the divorce statistics recently?'

'Well, what about the re-marriage statistics?' she retorted. 'If it is such an awful, unsuccessful institution why do people go into it over and over again? Why on earth don't the statisticians take that into account? I get the feeling sometimes that statistics are used quite ruthlessly in different ways to satisfy different arguments.'

'Of course they are.' He gave a sardonic smile. 'But since you'll be relying on them to substantiate your research during the next year you'll probably do the same.'

'I intend to be scrupulously fair,' Maisy told him fervently, and was rewarded with another smile— a genuine one this time, and one which made his angled, obdurate face look attractively relaxed.

'I'm pleased to hear it,' he murmured. 'And the point I was trying to make about this clinic was that when people are denied what they consider to be a God-given right it makes them extremely vulnerable. We see women coming in here who feel real failures. Men who feel less than men. Emasculated.'

'But that's crazy!' cried Maisy involuntarily.

He shook his head. 'Intellectually unsound, perhaps, but emotionally I would have said it was quite an understandable reaction.'

Maisy stared at him, instinct telling her that she could be certain of one thing. That Matthew Gallagher would not need to reproduce in order to feel a real man. Again she shivered but he did not appear to notice and just carried on speaking in that deep, calm voice.

'And there is terrific pressure on couples to reproduce—from would-be grandparents and from siblings and from peers. Particularly,' and for the first time the dark, shuttered features opened up with a kind of ardour as he tackled what was clearly one of his pet subjects, 'particularly in the nineties.'

He paused for a moment and Maisy found that she was holding her breath for more. 'Go on,' she said, fascinated. 'What's so special about the nineties?'

He threw her a considering look. 'Fashions change and so do lifestyles,' he said. 'Children and families are now seen as the ultimate possessions. Pick up any glossy magazine today and you'll find spread after spread of stars showing off their children. Twenty or even ten years ago they probably would have been denying they had been *married*, and yet now they can't wait to tell the world. Babies are big,' he finished. 'And if you don't have them you might consider yourself diminished in society's eyes.'

'How very cynical,' observed Maisy.

'What is?' he shot back, his dark brows furrowing.

'The idea that people only want children so that they can treat them like accessories—'

'You're missing the point completely!' he exploded. 'Of *course* people love their children once they have them—there's just a hell of a lot more pressure to have them these days! In the past, when a baby didn't appear, people tended to shrug and decide that it was meant to be. But nowadays we have the technology to dramatically increase their chances of having babies. Which is why they are willing, if not eager, to submit themselves to the most intimate questions and embarrassing tests and procedures ever devised by the medical profession.

'Investigation and treatment takes them through the mill and back,' he continued, 'so I want to make it easy on them. Stress makes a difficult situation even more difficult. Anxiety hinders conception— it's been proved time and time again. When my patients walk in here, Dr Jackson, I want it to be an oasis of calm for them. I want them to have supreme confidence in this clinic and in the staff's ability to aid their chances of conceiving.'

Maisy was shaken and more than a little moved by the depth of his feelings for his patients and the lucid way he had put his point over, expressing so beautifully what she had often thought herself. And how very frustrating to be in total accord with a man who was so loathsome!

But he was scanning her face searchingly, as if he was waiting for some sort of reply. 'I understand, Dr Gallagher,' she said in a low voice.

'Do you?'

She blinked under the intensity of that green stare. 'Of course.'

'Then don't ever be late again—not unless you have an iron-cast excuse for doing so. And smarten yourself up, too,' he added critically, his gaze raking over her. 'Looking scruffy makes you look disorganised. You are a representative of this clinic and, therefore, if *you* look disorganised patients will start fretting about whether their blood samples are being sent off on time or left to clot uselessly on a forgotten counter somewhere.'

Maisy was still smarting from the way he had found fault with her appearance and the fact that it was a justified criticism did not lessen the blow. 'You make your patients sound remarkably well informed,' she told him crossly.

It was quite the wrong thing to say. His face, which before had been merely disdainful, now grew dark with the kind of quietly controlled rage Maisy had only ever seen once before.

And that had been the weekend her brother, Benedict, had come home and told them all that he had a five-year-old daughter.

'Don't you ever dare patronise my patients,' he told her icily. 'Or underestimate their ability to understand their treatment. *Or* deny them their rights to know what is happening to them every step of the way. And never forget that the people we deal with daily are, for the most part, perfectly healthy. Just because their bodies are not performing what we consider to be a normal function does not make them invalids. Do I make myself understood, Dr Jackson?'

'Absolutely,' she managed to bite out, though she

was almost shaking with rage at being spoken to like that. Why, even as the lowliest of medical students getting in the way on some tyrant of a sister's ward she couldn't ever remember someone being so rude to her!

'Good,' he said, and glanced down at his desk, his attention caught by a neat pile of letters awaiting his signature.

He seemed to have forgotten that she was there, and Maisy watched in silence while he sighed ten letters, before pulling herself together enough to say coolly, 'Just what would you like me to do now, Dr Gallagher?'

He looked up from the last letter he had signed with a flourish, and narrowed his eyes. 'You will come to Theatre and observe me while I do the morning's embryo transfers,' he answered. 'That way you will see precisely how I like things done. And who knows? You might even learn something.' But the tone of his closing remark was doubtful.

And as Maisy followed the tall, dark Australian out of his consulting room she thought that the pursuit of knowledge had never seemed quite so daunting.

CHAPTER THREE

MATTHEW GALLAGHER strode down the corridor towards Theatres at a fantastic pace, and Maisy almost had to run to keep up with him, trying to take everything in as he shot out comments like, 'That's the lab over there,' and, 'That's the co-ordinating room,' and, 'Over there is the counselling room.'

'Is there much of that?' queried Maisy with interest.

'Much of what?' he frowned.

'Counselling,' she said sweetly, wondering if he was always this stubbornly obtuse.

'We do a great deal,' he answered swiftly. 'We go in for counselling of would-be patients in a big way in this unit.'

'I'd like to learn more about that,' said Maisy, who had won the psychology prize in her year at medical school.

'You will,' he promised, looking slightly mollified at her enthusiasm as he continued to tear along the corridor.

At one point, however, he completely surprised her by slowing down and saying, 'Do you know very much about the kind of work we do here?'

She suspected that she might have said yes if she hadn't been speaking to someone as exacting and

31

passionate about his subject as Matthew Gallagher. He was the kind of man who, she suspected, would easily catch you out if you made spurious claims to knowledge!

'Not much,' she admitted, in a low voice. 'Only general stuff which I read up—'

'The week before you came here, I expect?' he queried, with a spark of unexpected humour.

'My last job didn't leave me with a lot of time for reading,' commented Maisy drily.

'Birmingham City General?'

Maisy asked the question without thinking about it. 'How did you know that?'

The withering look which had chased the humour away was no more than she deserved. 'I've hardly discovered the meaning of life,' he said coolly, his step now totally in tune with hers. 'I read your references, as any consultant would. Now, why don't you tell me what you know about this unit?' he instructed.

'I know that you concentrate mainly on IVF,' said Maisy and, seeing his questioning look, added wryly, 'which stands for *in vitro* fertilisation. You surely weren't imagining that I didn't know the meaning of IVF, Dr Gallagher?'

He shrugged. 'My years in medicine have taught me never to take anything—or anyone, for that matter—for granted. I've worked with junior surgeons whom I wouldn't trust to sew a button on straight! But that's beside the point. Tell me what *in vitro* fertilisation means, will you? Oh, and I guess you'd better call me Matthew,' he added reluctantly.

'Maisy,' she added, feeling oddly shy.

'Maisy,' he repeated slowly, as if he had never said the word before. 'Very English,' he observed. 'We don't have many Maisys in Australia.'

'They're all called Sheila, I suppose?' she queried, with deadpan innocence.

He actually smiled. '*Touché*. But actually I'm going to call you Jackson.'

Maisy's face remained impassive, showing nothing of the flicker of irritation his words had provoked. 'Why?' she demanded crisply.

'It suits you better,' came the succinct, mocking response.

'I see,' Maisy observed slowly as the flicker of irritation grew into a fair-sized flame, but still she didn't react. She certainly didn't like him referring to her by her surname alone. With its boarding-school connotations, it made her feel less than feminine. But to tell Matthew Gallagher that would be an admission of vulnerability, wouldn't it? And right now she needed a display of vulnerability like a hole in the head. So she fixed him with a prim expression and said nothing.

He narrowed his eyes. 'Meanwhile, I'm still waiting for you to explain what *in vitro* fertilisation means, Jackson,' he told her softly. 'Pretend I'm a first-year student. See if that helps.'

It was a ludicrous request since Maisy's imagination failed dramatically to come to her rescue. Had he ever been a student, she wondered, with all a student's insecurities? She couldn't ever imagine him lanky or spotty. Still less blushing and broke and lacking in confidence.

He was wearing a pale green shirt and exquisitely cut cream-coloured chinos, and carried with him all the quiet self-assurance of a man who has *always* been absolutely gorgeous.

Maisy swallowed as she tried not to dwell on the image of just *how* gorgeous. 'IVF means fertilisation outside the body,' she told him quickly. 'And in the United Kingdom all IVF treatment clinics are monitored and licensed by the Human Fertilisation and Embryology Authority—the HFEA—which is a public body set up by an Act of Parliament.'

He raised his eyebrows. 'I'm impressed,' he murmured.

'Elementary,' said Maisy, trying her best not to sound smug.

'I do embryo transfers every Monday morning and Friday afternoon,' he said. 'What do you know about that?'

Maisy stood aside to let a hurrying lab technician get past her. 'Only what I've read,' she smiled, and Matthew Gallagher suddenly found himself trans-fixed by the wide innocence of that smile and frowned.

'Then tell me what you've read,' he instructed in a growling voice.

Maisy racked her brains to describe embryo trans-fer as simply as possible. 'The patient has an intensive and fairly complex drug regime from day one of her cycle. This includes an injection of progesterone to mature the eggs in the follicle. Once

the woman's eggs *are* mature she is taken to Theatre
and the fertility specialist visualises the ovaries. This
is done either under a general anaesthetic or with
sedation and analgesia.'

'Good.'

'The specialist then punctures each follicle and
flushes out the eggs into a sealed test-tube. As soon
as the tube is full a nurse takes it to the embryologist,
where he mixes it in a dish with the man's concen-
trated and washed sperm.'

'And then?'

'Then the dish is left in the incubator until the
following morning, and if fertilisation has occurred
then we report back to the couple and arrange for
the embryo to be transferred to the patient.'

'Which is what we are about to do this morning,'
he said, giving her a small nod of recognition. 'That
was a very concise description, Jackson.'

'Why, thank you, Matthew,' she murmured drily,
glancing around her with interest.

'It's a small unit,' he elaborated, with obvious
pleasure, 'but our success rate is exciting a lot of
interest among the bigger London hospitals.'

Maisy nodded. 'I saw the comparative figures in
last month's leader in the *British Medical Journal*,'
she said, remembering the night she had forced herself to look at it, her eyelids nearly dropping down
so often that in the end she had stood up to read it
to prevent herself from falling asleep!

He threw her a look of frank surprise. 'You *have*
been doing your homework, Jackson!'

Maisy stopped dead in her tracks in the middle

of the corridor and decided that Dr Matthew Gallagher was really going to have to rethink his attitude towards her. 'Now look here!' She shook her head with indignation so that the wheaten curls flopped around her face. 'I *may* have turned up late this morning! And I may not be currently topping the hospital's best-dressed list! But I've read the *British Medical Journal* since my very first day in med school,' she informed him angrily, 'so I'd appreciate it if you didn't patronise me, Dr Gallagher!'

'Matthew,' he corrected, tongue-in-cheek, but Maisy was so angry that she took him literally.

'I shall call you Dr Gallagher if I want!' she declared savagely since he had not asked *her* permission before he had started referring to her by her surname! 'And just because I'm a woman please don't imagine that my knowledge is patchy *or* that I try to get by on feminine wiles alone—because I don't!'

'No,' he said slowly, his eyes flicking from the top of her wild, wheat-blonde hair all the way down to where her khaki suede shoes clashed horribly with her navy culottes. 'No. I don't imagine that you do. . .'

It was the most damning thing that anyone had ever said to her and Maisy was filled with a twofold desire—not to react at all, and to *really* pull the stops out next time she saw him!

In the days before Giles had shattered most of her confidence she had had men trying to eat out of her hand or, rather, trying to lure her into their beds. Trying being the operative word, of course. Because no one, apart from her ex-fiancé, had ever suceeeded. And even that victory, which Giles had fought so hard for, had been a dramatic failure. As he had reminded her with a chilling regularity which had finally made Maisy come to her senses. . .

In silence they walked past a large red sign and then, with a sigh of what sounded like relief, Matthew said, 'Here's Theatre. We'd better get cracking; we're running behind.'

'Must be the pep-talk you gave me,' said Maisy casually, determined to pretend that his earlier remark about feminine wiles had not hurt her. . . But it *had* hurt her. . .

He stared down at her, and as their eyes met in a fusion of grey and green hers dared him to condemn her for giving as good as she got. Rebellion surged through her body like electricity. Let him try, she thought wildly, aware of the sudden, erratic thumping of her heart. Let him just *try*!

Because if he thought that she was going to spend the next six months with him speaking to her as if she were some kind of white-bellied insect who had just crawled from underneath the nearest stone instead of as a colleague and an equal then he had another think coming!

But again he surprised her when he said, with an almost gentle push on her elbow, 'Calm down, Jackson. Calm down. The women's changing room is through there. I'll see you in Theatre in two minutes. OK?'

'O-OK,' she mumbled gratefully, thinking that

her self-esteem must be at an all-time low if she proved to be such a sucker for a few soft words!

Maisy glanced at her watch and rushed into the changing room for the fastest two minutes she had ever experienced. She really had to push it to make it in the time he had allotted to her but she didn't dare risk being late. Not twice in one day!

Fortunately, she found a nurse to ask which locker she should take, and as the nurse was about a million times more friendly than Samantha Marsh had been it was a mollified Maisy who stripped off her clothes, donned trousers and overshirt and hurried into Theatre.

She found herself confronted by the sight of Matthew's broad-shouldered frame, wearing the traditional theatre uniform of dark green cotton trousers and short-sleeved top as he scrubbed at the sink. For a moment she just stood still and stared at him.

He looked round and saw her. 'Hurry up,' was all he said, but not unkindly.

Maisy had scrubbed for more cases than she had eaten hot dinners so why did she suddenly feel acutely shy? Surely not because of the way he looked? Yes, Matthew Gallagher *was* a very attractive man, but he was by no means the first attractive man she had worked with. Why, she had been engaged to a man who had been popularly known as the Hospital Heart Throb!

So why the rapid pulse? The insistent rise of colour to her cheeks? Why on earth were the tips of her breasts stinging, as though they were raw and someone had just thrown icy antiseptic all over them?

He's just washing his hands, she told herself woodenly, not doing a slow striptease to try and tantalise you!

The very idea of Matthew Gallagher doing a slow striptease actually brought a smile to her lips and, unknown to Maisy, the tall man at her side noticed it.

As her lips curved into a bow Matthew found himself stiffening very slightly for reasons he did not even attempt to fathom. Instead, he put them down with a kind of weary cynicism to the ever-present threat of sexual attraction.

Which was bound to crop up when men and women worked in such close, tense situations as hospitals, he reasoned. Even if the woman in question clearly couldn't be bothered to brush her hair properly. Or to dress decently.

Matthew suppressed a contemptuous shudder.

Apart from his strict rule about not dating people he worked with, his exacting standards spilled over into his social life, too. And he was handsome enough never to have had to compromise those standards. He liked a woman to look like a woman— all perfumed and sweet and feminine. And not as though she had just crawled through a hedge backwards.

And he liked a woman to *act* like a woman, too. Soft and giving and compliant—not spiky and indignant like his latest research assistant!

Meanwhile, Maisy was picking up the mixed messages he was sending out as she carefully and obsessively scrubbed her hands and arms—all the way up to her elbows—in the way that doctors in every country in the world were taught.

She looked up to discover that the secretive green eyes were narrowed at her with a thoughtful kind of scrutiny which somehow was not in the least bit flattering. A tingle of attraction began to fizz infuriatingly down her spine, and she shook the excess water off her hands with a flourish.

He disapproved of her, of that she was certain.

Well, so what?

She stared back, her expression telling him in no uncertain terms that she neither cared for, nor was searching for, any sort of approval other than the purely professional kind.

Maisy hid a smile as she pulled on her gloves, not missing the somewhat startled look which had momentarily crossed those ruggedly handsome features.

He simply wasn't used to women who didn't fawn over him, she realised with glee, and vowed to spend the next six months being as cool as cucumber towards him!

'Bring the first case in,' he said, flashing a devastating smile at the nurse, who visibly melted under its impact.

And left Maisy realising that keeping her cool when faced with a smile like that might be more difficult than she had anticipated!

The first patient was wheeled in, fully conscious, her adoring partner clutching her hand as though it were held there by super-glue.

Matthew smiled at the woman and Maisy couldn't help noticing the effect that his smile seemed to have on everyone—not just the nurses. It was, she thought—even while she despised herself for thinking it—just like the sun coming out.

'Hello, Mrs Sergeant,' Matthew said. 'And Mr Sergeant. All set?'

'All set!' they chorused, with determinedly cheerful expressions pinned to their faces.

Mrs Sergeant was an attractive woman with thick, blue-black hair who smiled back at Matthew, but the fine lines of strain around her blue eyes made Maisy suspect that this was not the first time she had undergone treatment for infertility.

'This is Dr Jackson,' Matthew was saying. 'She has come to work here for a year. She's going to do some research that, in some small way, might make it easier for someone to have a baby. Aren't you, Jackson?'

His insulting manner of speaking to her momentarily forgotten, Maisy stared back at him wonderingly.

His eyes bored their message at her as he made his passionate and rather dramatic announcement and suddenly, like a bolt from the blue, some of his passion transferred itself to Maisy.

So simple, she thought, and yet so profound.

She found herself staring up at him, her grey eyes wide and—if only she knew it—very impressionable as she realised that, yes, it *was* possible. In fact, anything was possible.

It was like a revelation to Maisy.

Before that moment she had looked on her research year as one of having to read a lot of rather dry books and cobble together a few statistics and somehow to produce something from that. Something which was publishable. *Anything* which was publishable, to be more truthful! Another rung up the ladder towards her own eventual consultancy.

Hopefully.

But, in truth, as Matthew himself had pointed out so perceptively in his office, it had been the regular hours which had attracted her more than anything. Years of being on call and at the mercy of her ever-shrilling bleeper had left her with a fatigue which sometimes seemed bone-deep.

And yet now she suddenly felt ashamed of wanting to opt for an easy life.

For the first time in a long time—and certainly since the acrimony of her broken engagement— Maisy felt some of her zeal for the job return.

Mrs Sergeant was looking up at her with trusting eyes. 'Are you really, Doctor?'

And Maisy smiled. 'Yes, I am,' she answered softly. 'Or, at least, I'm going to give it the very best shot I've got.'

It was only slightly ruined by the sight of one of the technicians giving another a wry look which quite clearly spoke volumes about Matthew Gallagher's ability to get women eating out of his hand!

But Maisy didn't care. With a long, freckled finger she stroked the back of Mrs Sergeant's hand—ever mindful of the soothing effect that human contact had on patients who were worried. And Mrs Sergeant, despite the bright smile which she kept pinning to her mouth when she remembered, was looking very worried indeed.

As the nurse began helping Mrs Sergeant's legs into the high stirrups the patient clutched at Maisy's hand as if it were a lifeline.

'Can you make it work this time, Doctor?' she joked weakly.

Maisy looked directly into Matthew's eyes. 'Dr Gallagher is the expert. In fact, he's one of the world's leading specialists in this field. If anyone can make it work, he can.'

Matthew gave a flicker of a smile and Maisy was infuriated to discover that her pulse rate had quickened in response. She squeezed Mrs Sergeant's hand and forced herself not to think about how kiss-able his mouth looked when he smiled like that. 'This isn't your first embryo transfer, I take it?' she asked the patient.

Mrs Sergeant shook her shiny dark head. 'Heavens, no. I wish it was! This is my third time.' She bit her lip and looked up at Matthew anxiously. 'Isn't it, Doctor?'

'That's right,' he agreed neutrally as he took the embryo transfer catheter from the nurse at his side. 'So, fingers crossed!' From over the top of his mask the sage eyes crinkled encouragingly, and Mrs Sergeant looked up at him from the trolley with such clear hope and trust written on her face that Maisy found herself having to swallow down a great lump of emotion.

She watched in silence as he conducted the procedure while keeping up a running commentary for her benefit with all the non-intrusive fluency of the natural-born teacher.

He held up the embryo-transfer catheter to show her. 'These particular embryos have been frozen for several months,' he explained. 'As you know, we're only allowed to put three back by law—'

'Oh?' Maisy looked up with interest. 'Why?'

'Because this planet has enough problems with over-population as it is!' he declared, only half-jokingly. 'Also, there is always the chance that one or more of the embryos might divide into a twin pregnancy. A mother-to-be might then find herself looking at the prospect of having four babies minimum!'

'Sounds wonderful,' sighed Mrs Sergeant blissfully. 'Doesn't it, Scott?'

Her husband went a whiter shade of pale. 'Don't be fanciful, Angie,' he pleaded. 'We only have three bedrooms—remember?'

'And a multiple pregnancy can put both mother and foetuses at risk,' said Maisy quietly.

There was silence in Theatre as Dr Gallagher carefully passed the catheter up through the vagina. 'The embryos are loaded into the front of the catheter,' he told Maisy. 'And now I'm just going through the cervix and into the fundus. That's where I'm going to deposit them.' His brows knitted together in concentration. 'There!' he said after a moment or two. 'All done!'

Beside him stood the embryologist, who immediately took the catheter out of Theatre.

Then Matthew pulled off his gloves and gave Mrs Sergeant's hand a quick squeeze. 'Right, Angie,' he said with a smile. 'Nurse will wheel you back now. I'd like you to continue lying down for an hour—let's give that baby a fighting chance. Then Dr Jackson and I will come and see you before you go. OK?'

'OK,' responded the woman on a tremulous whisper, her beautiful eyes bright with emotion. 'I just don't know how to thank you.'

'That's easy. By relaxing and taking care of yourself,' he told her. 'Promise?'

'I promise,' she answered with a smile as her husband and the porter began to push the trolley out of Theatre.

Maisy and Matthew walked over to the sink to prepare for the next patient.

'Anything you want to ask me?' he queried as he turned the tap on full blast and let it power over his muscular arms.

Maisy helped herself to a dollop of antiseptic soap. 'Why does the embryologist take the catheter away?' she asked him.

'He takes it back to the laboratory and examines it to check that no embryos have been left stuck to the side of the catheter. We never forget the moral and ethical implications of just what we're dealing with,' he said.

'What—you mean that in the catheter you have human life itself? And not just a bunch of cells?' Maisy questioned slowly.

He nodded and turned to survey her thoughtfully. 'Absolutely.'

Their eyes met, and at that precise moment— professionally, at least—they were in total accord.

Once again Maisy felt something close to desire shivering its way down her spine. An odd bitter-sweet kind of longing she had never experienced before—the kind of sensation you simultaneously wanted to cling like mad to and yet to run from its danger and its potency.

Seeing her body tremble like that, Matthew instinctively found that he was holding his breath. Deliberately he moved his head by a fraction, which meant that she was no longer directly in his line of vision, but still he had to make a conscious effort to force his mind back to what he was *supposed* to be thinking about.

Work.

He flattened his mouth into its habitual hard line. 'Are you aware, Dr Jackson, that we usually only make three attempts to implant an embryo?'

Wondering what had caused him to look so brooding all of a sudden, Maisy watched the movement of his hands as he soaped them laboriously. Strong, yet delicate, she found herself thinking, a true surgeon's hands. 'I wasn't, no,' she answered, dragging her thoughts into line with his. 'Why is that?'

'Because we would prefer to investigate *why* the procedure isn't working,' answered Matthew, suddenly aware that he could smell some subtle sort of flowery, soapy smell which clung to her warm skin.

He moved even further away from her and surveyed her almost sternly.

'You see, we never forget that the entire process of assisted conception is emotionally and physically very draining, particularly, of course, for the woman.' He shook droplets of water off his hands. 'Added to which, the financial costs of repeated treatments can be astronomical, and we are acutely aware of our responsibility to the patient. At this clinic we guard fiercely against the possibility of exploitation—'

Maisy looked up. 'Oh?'

His green eyes were intense. 'Patients caught up in the emotional roller coaster which is fertility treatment are often tempted to keep trying a particular treatment—even if it has shown no sign of working so far. An unscrupulous clinic could allow them to do so. We do not.'

'And would that be so very bad?' queried Maisy. 'If the couple could afford to keep paying?'

He shook his dark head. 'Yes, it would,' came his unequivocal reply, 'because there has to be some sort of balance if people are to live fulfilled lives. And, quite apart from the physical toll that fertility treatment puts on a woman's health and well-being, the psychological implications of repeated and unsuccessful attempts are immense.'

'In what way?' asked Maisy interestedly.

'Think about it,' he told her brutally. 'When reproduction becomes your *raison d'être* it affects your life in so many ways.'

Maisy stared up at him with curious eyes. 'You

mean, you become obsessed with temperature charts and ovulation times—that kind of thing?'

He gave a tiny, impatient shake of the head. 'That is a small part of it, yes, but the hidden agenda is that the act of intercourse primarily becomes about making a baby instead of about expressing love within the relationship.'

It was the first time in her medical career that Maisy felt unable to remain objective. It suddenly seemed impossible to find the necessary detachment to be able to discuss such intimate subjects as love-making without getting embarrassed by it. And to discuss them with a blazingly attractive man whom she suddenly found herself unable to look in the eyes.

Maisy felt the blush long before she was sure it must have manifested itself on her face. It lingered at the area behind her ears and prickled at the roots of her hair, before spreading inexorably in two heated flares across her cheeks.

Matthew saw her rapid rise in colour, and if it had been any other female member of his staff he might have felt relaxed enough to make a joke of it and thus lighten the atmosphere.

But he did not feel in the slightest bit relaxed—quite the contrary, in fact. He felt uptight and suspicious and. . . A muscle clenched convulsively in his cheek as he reluctantly allowed himself to acknowledge the potent power of sexual attraction.

And yet he most emphatically did *not* find this woman in the least bit desirable, he told himself savagely. In fact, if he had drawn up a list of his ten top female attributes he doubted whether Maisy Jackson would have possessed *any* of them.

But if that *was* the case why was he suddenly experiencing the most bizarre and unnerving yearning to pull her into his arms and to press his mouth down, hard, on those soft, yielding lips?

He made a small, terse exclamation of annoyance. He had been without a woman for too long, yes. He was intelligent enough to realise *that*. And he had had strong personal reasons for his self-imposed celibacy. Did he need a woman so badly that even this pale and freckle-faced creature with the wild hair and stormy grey eyes could manage to heat the blood in his loins?

His mouth twisted as he remembered the drug rep who had visited him in the department last week. She had been an ice-cool designer-clad cookie who had, nonetheless, boldly invited him to have dinner with her one evening. He had smiled and given a noncommittal shrug. But why? Maybe he should take her up on her invitation. . .

Maisy's breath caught in her throat as she read something inexplicably exciting in the sudden darkening of his eyes and the sudden tension in his face. 'Is. . .anything wrong, Matthew?' she whispered, wondering why her voice was sounding so strangely husky and why it should shake so vulnerably when she pronounced his name.

Oh, for heaven's sake, Maisy Jackson, she told herself impatiently, pull yourself together before you make a *complete* fool of yourself.

'Our next patient will be here any minute,' he

announced abruptly, and just as curtly walked across the theatre and away from her, leaving Maisy wondering whether she had in some way offended him.

And making her doubly determined never to let his undeniable sex appeal get through her defences again.

CHAPTER FOUR

BUT by five o'clock that afternoon Maisy was past caring whether or not she had offended the brilliant but emotionally mercurial Dr Gallagher—she was too busy scolding herself for her naïvety.

Had she really been labouring under the illusion that doing a nine-to-five research job would be some sort of *rest*? Perhaps if she had been working in any department other than the one headed by the autocratic Australian then it might have been. But, *really*, she had not stopped working all day.

Or learning, she reminded herself. He might be an exacting, tryannical perfectionist but he was a brilliant tutor, too.

Lunch had been of the grabbed-sandwich variety. After the last of the embryo transfers in Theatre, Matthew had told her to meet him in the unit's co-ordination room.

'That's where the team has meetings,' he'd explained when he'd seen her frown. 'Call it our office, if you like. All the doctors and nurses get together there over coffee to thrash out issues which concern us. Oh, and to have lunch,' he added, with what was almost a smile. 'So be there as quickly as you can—or there won't bc anything left!'

It was not as though Maisy was unrealistic. Her father was a doctor, her mother a nurse. Her big brother was now a consultant and her sister was a midwife. She *knew* what hospital life was like.

Nevertheless, when she walked into the co-ordination room and saw that what Matthew had meant by 'lunch' was, in fact, two curled-up and dried-out egg and cress sandwiches her chin nearly hit the floor.

Matthew looked up from the newspaper, which was spread all over his lap, and shrugged when he saw her face. 'I did tell you to be quick,' he murmured, with a rueful glance at the almost empty plate. 'What kept you?'

Severe dysmenorrhoea, that was what, but she certainly wasn't going to tell Matthew Gallagher *that*! Maisy had suffered from painful periods since her late teens, and they seemed to have been getting worse and worse lately.

And while the medic in her knew that she ought to see her own doctor about them she was also acting true to Jackson family form. Her brother, Ben, had taken his finals whilst enduring the racking pain of an infected wisdom tooth—and passed—whilst her mother had been out digging up potatoes just minutes before giving birth to her first child!

Never had the saying 'Physician, heal thyself' been more appropriate, but Maisy had so far stubbornly refused to heed it.

Matthew was frowning. 'You look awfully pale. You're not about to faint on me, are you?'

Perhaps it was his total lack of concern which did it. The fact that he hadn't left her any decent sandwiches. The fact that he couldn't *really* care less how she felt. All he was bothered about was that she might leave *him* short-staffed. Maisy bared her teeth like a tigress.

'*You*, Dr Gallagher,' she said, with far more venom than was strictly necessary, 'are the last person in the world I would dream of fainting on!'

The cynical and disbelieving elevation of his eyebrows told her that she was in danger of being judged a hysterical female. 'I was speaking metaphorically, rather than literally, Jackson,' he chided sarcastically.

'Oh, were you?' Her face was mutinous.

'Mmm.' He seemed to lose all interest then, returning his attention instead to his newspaper and waving a desultory hand in front of the plate. 'Better grab what's left, hadn't you? We don't have a lot of time. There's coffee in the percolator.'

Maisy unenthusiastically surveyed the wilting bits of green cress which were escaping from the soggy egg filling.

It was more than the fact that eating those grotty sandwiches did not appeal one little bit. It was a question of pride. Eating his disgusting leftovers would be a symbolic gesture of capitulation to his surly bad-temperedness! 'I'm not hungry,' said Maisy tightly.

Now she had his attention again, but this time his expression looked positively black.

'You ought to eat.'

'Is that an order, Dr Gallagher?'

'What an extraordinary question!' he observed coolly. 'Why? Do you associate the consumption of food with power, Dr Jackson? And isn't that a touch dangerous? It's what anorexics do, isn't it?' The sage eyes unhurriedly surveyed her slim but healthy curves. 'Though, I must say, you don't *look* as if you have problems relating to food.'

'I'm not really up for amateur psychology sessions in my lunch-hour,' she returned repressively.

'Nor for eating either?' he queried, his lip curving with unspoken censure. 'Then may I enquire what it is that you *usually* do in your lunch-hour?'

The gleam in the enigmatic eyes and the sardonic little half-smile which curved his mouth made Maisy quickly realise just what it was he was suggesting and, to her horror, she felt a repeat of the blush which had plagued her earlier in Theatre.

It was the very last straw.

On top of the griping cramps which were like iron-bands across her stomach and a very low blood sugar caused by not having eaten Maisy completely lost her temper.

'Well, it isn't what you think!' she stormed.

He put the paper down. 'And what do I think?'

'You know damned well what you think! That's the trouble with you men!' she raged loudly, now completely at the mercy of her hormones and her memories of her ex-fiancé. 'All you ever think about is sex, sex, sex!'

There was a stunned silence. All the remaining colour went from Maisy's face as she realised just what it was she had said.

And to whom.

Meanwhile Matthew surveyed her thoughtfully.

What had just occurred was strictly unprofessional. She should not have shouted at him like that, and she certainly should not have made the inference that she had done.

But was he completely blameless?

Had he not prompted her outburst by himself implying that she spent her lunch-hours in far more passionate pursuits than eating dried-up sandwiches?

And, besides, Matthew had spent most of his working life with women. He had been one of Australian's finest obstetricians and gynaecologists before he had become a fertility specialist. He knew women. He knew their mood swings. How often they were at the mercy of fluctuating hormone levels. And, unless he was very much mistaken, all was not well with Maisy Jackson.

He found himself looking at her ringless fingers, his sharp eyes immediately detecting the faint white circle on her left ring finger. Had a wedding band recently lain in place there? he wondered. Was Maisy Jackson newly divorced? He sneaked a glance at her clear, unlined skin, untouched by make-up. She looked about twenty, he thought suddenly, though he knew that could not be so. But even so surely not old enough to be divorced?

He stifled a small sigh of irritation. Just because she was a woman didn't mean that she had to bring all her problems to work with her, now did it?

Very deliberately Matthew folded up the newspaper and carefully placed it on the coffee-table

while he collected his thoughts. Whatever her provo-
cation—or his part in it—the conversation must be
abruptly terminated and forgotten if he was to have
no repetition of this kind of behaviour.

His face took on a forbidding mask, so much so
that one of the secretaries who had walked into the
room took one look at him and immediately walked
out again!

'Spare me the histrionics, Dr Jackson,' he said
coldly. 'Just make sure you have the stamina for a
busy afternoon ahead—quite how you achieve it
really does not interest me in the slightest.' He stood
up. 'I have to make a couple of phone calls. Then
I'll be back.'

And, miserably, knowing that he had only spoken
sense, Maisy waited until he had left the room and
then wolfed down the two sandwiches and drank a
cup of coffee so thick with sugar that she could
have stood her spoon up in it!

Her afternoon had been spent sitting in and
observing while Matthew had seen the new cases
which had been referred to him—but even that had
begun badly.

The two of them had been in his office after that
unfortunate 'lunch', with Matthew busy scrawling
his signature over yet another stack of letters—
which this time had been almost as high as the Eiffel
Tower—while Maisy had attempted to make some
sense of the stodgy scientific paper he had given
her to read.

Normally, despite the disparaging remarks she
had made about them earlier, she found statistics as

easy to handle as ABC. But, then, she didn't *normally* have over six feet of spectacular male perfection sitting just inches away from her and totally distracting her.

Her eyes were just scanning page one for the third time when he looked up, the mysterious green eyes hooded.

'Bored?' he snapped.

'Why do you ask?' she snapped back defensively.

'You've read the same page three times, that's why.'

She was in a dilemma. Did she tell him the truth? But how shaming for *her*—and how ego-building for *him*—if she admitted that the words looked like hieroglyphics because she was so flustered by his presence!

Crossing her fingers, which were hidden in the pocket of her white coat, she decided to prevaricate.

'It isn't the *best* piece of work I've seen on the subject,' she murmured, with what she hoped sounded like authority.

'Oh? Care to elaborate?'

Since she hadn't taken in a single word of it, she had to make a wild stab at criticising it! 'It isn't what I'd call reader-*friendly*,' she told him truthfully, embracing a subject which happened to be very dear to her heart. 'Just because a paper is written for academics and scientists and doctors doesn't mean that it has to be as dry as dust, does it? However good the piece, it won't impress *anyone* if it's designed to make the reader nod off because the language is so stuffy.'

An indecipherable light gleamed from the depths of his green eyes. 'And you think you can do better?'

Maisy shrugged, wondering how she could get out of his challenge without appearing to back down. 'I can try.'

'Do,' came his cool response.

'Just out of interest, w-who wrote it?' Maisy asked, with a heart-clenching suspicion.

'I did,' he said, without lifting his dark head, but Maisy could have *sworn* that she detected the faintest undercurrent of amusement in his reply. 'Ask the first patients to come in, will you, Jackson?'

With cheeks as red as the Chinese flag, Maisy walked unsteadily out of Matthew's consulting room and into the waiting room to find that in a very short time it had filled up with men and women who, without exception, sat as couples, very close together.

Several of the women, who looked as though they were in their mid-thirties, were even clutching their partner's hands with the kind of possessive insecurity usually associated with teenagers.

But, there again, thought Maisy fleetingly, the great highs and lows of emotion often displayed by teenagers were not exclusive to them. Adults were often highly demonstrative, too. It was just *she* who had the problem and wouldn't—*couldn't*—show passion.

And hadn't Giles just taken immense pleasure in reminding her of that fact? she remembered bitterly.

As well as being in neat pairs, the men and women differed from the occupants of most of the other hospital waiting rooms in that they all looked perfectly healthy. And Maisy was reminded of Matthew's words about not regarding people with fertility problems as invalids.

Her heart sank when she saw the back of Staff Nurse Marsh's dark, glossy head on the opposite side of the waiting room, and hoped that she wasn't going to have a repeat performance of this morning's unwelcoming response.

But Maisy took one look at the nurse's unsmiling face as she turned around and realised that she looked even grumpier than she had done earlier.

Well, she was *not* going to be intimidated!

Ignoring the brief, appalled glance which the nurse sent in the direction of her awry hair, Maisy cleared her throat. 'Could you ask the first patient to come into Dr Gallagher's office, please, Staff?' she asked crisply.

Staff Nurse Marsh gave Maisy another look which bordered on the insolent. 'Certainly, Doctor. I'll bring them in myself. I always chaperon Dr Gallagher.'

She was making it sound like some sort of erotic love pact! thought Maisy crossly. 'That won't be necessary today,' she said and then, as she saw the sharp look of distress on the nurse's face, she added gently, 'If I'm in there, learning the ropes, it seems a bit of a waste of time to have you in there too. Isn't there something else you could be doing?'

'What—like scrubbing out a few bedpans, you mean?' demanded Nurse Marsh shrilly.

'That wasn't what I meant at all!' retorted Maisy,

stung, and before she could prevent herself added, 'And I am not used to having my authority questioned in such a way—'

'By a nurse?' prompted Nurse Marsh stonily.

'By *anyone*!' Maisy snapped back, not hearing the door open and close very quietly behind her. 'I know I'm new here and I've never worked in an infertility clinic before so obviously I'm going to be at a disadvantage for a while. But I would like to feel that I can count on your help, Staff Nurse, not your hindrance. Do you understand?'

'Y-yes, Dr Jackson.'

To Maisy's astonishment, Nurse Marsh's face suddenly took on a look of browbeaten terror. Her bottom lip had begun to tremble like a child's and she looked as if she was just about to burst into a full flood of tears. She was overreacting like mad to what seemed to Maisy like a perfectly justified admonishment. Why? she wondered briefly.

And then the deep voice from directly behind her illuminated the reasoning behind Nurse Marsh's Oscar-winning performance.

'I thought I told you to ask Staff Nurse to show the first patient in?' said Matthew Gallagher in an oddly quiet sort of voice as he gave a frowning look at both women. 'Is something the matter?'

The bottom lip wobbled like an unset jelly. 'I-it's j-just. . .'

'Just what, Samantha?' prompted Matthew gently, thinking that this really was most uncharacteristic behaviour from the normally confident and attractive staff nurse.

Samantha shook her glossy head. 'N-nothing.'

Matthew gave a small click of impatience. 'I'm not a mind-reader!' he snapped. 'And I don't see how I can possibly hope to help solve any problems if you don't tell me what they are!'

'Just that Dr Jackson told me that I wasn't to chaperon you, Matthew,' said Nurse Marsh, looking even more outraged and hurt.

There was a moment of angry silence.

'Oh, *did* she?' asked Matthew dangerously, and threw Maisy a smouldering look of exasperation. 'Well, Samantha *always* chaperons me—'

Oh, I'll bet she does, thought Maisy, her grey eyes narrowing. How very cosy!

'—and I do not propose changing my routine now,' snarled Matthew. 'Neither will I allow *you* to make any changes without first consulting me, Dr Jackson! Particularly on your first day, and given your inexperience.' His eyes glinted with anger. 'However, I do not propose lecturing you in my preferred methods of work. Not now, with a waiting room full of anxious people. So, can I please have the first patients in? *Now*, Samantha?'

'Yes, Matthew,' murmured Nurse Marsh huskily, and as he turned to stride back into his consulting room she slanted a look of pure triumph at Maisy as she said, 'Mr and Mrs Richards to see Dr Gallagher, please.'

As the first couple was shown into the consulting room Maisy was forced to endure the humiliation of watching Matthew and Samantha interact like a well-worn double act.

And—she had to admit—it was pretty amazing stuff to watch.

Matthew did not ever have to ask his staff nurse for any instrument, notes—anything. Everything he could possibly need was laid precisely to hand. Like a well-trained servant, she anticipated his every need in a way which Maisy might have found admirable had the other woman not found it necessary to send a smug look of victory across at her whenever Matthew had his back turned.

And Maisy had to admit that whatever Matthew's shortcomings were where staff relations were concerned he was absolutely *brilliant* at handling patients.

When the fourth set of patients was ushered in the woman, who was sensibly dressed in flat shoes and a long, flowing dress, burst into tears as soon as she sat down.

Unlike some doctors Maisy had sat in on in the past, Matthew offered no critical and useless advice such as telling her to pull herself together.

Instead, he just let her cry and cry. Only when the cries had become snuffles did he say in a quiet and gentle voice, 'Want to tell me all about it?'

'Yes, Doctor!' she wailed disconsolately, then announced in between sniffs, 'I can't have a baby!'

'Well, we don't know that yet for sure, do we?' interjected Matthew softly, and fixed her with a soft green stare. 'These are very early days indeed, Mrs Barnes, and even if there *are* problems with conceiving that doesn't mean that you can't have a baby. There are so many options open to us these days, and we haven't explored any of them yet.'

Mrs Barnes shook her head, as though he had not spoken. 'And do you know one of the worst things about the whole business, Doctor, is that I'm such an earth mother at heart! Aren't I, Adam?' She fixed her husband with a sharp look.

Adam, who seemed to wear a permanant look of agreement, nodded his head benignly. 'Oh, yes, dear.'

'Or, rather, I'm waiting to be an earth mother! We live in the country, we're virtually self-sufficient and last year I gave up my job to have the family we've always dreamed about. Waiting, just waiting to fill our house with children. And now we can't!'

Matthew nodded and offered her a box of tissues, but the woman shook her head and as she withdrew a huge, crumpled cotton handkerchief from her handbag. 'No, thanks, Dr Gallagher,' she sniffed. 'Let's do the planet a good turn and save a tree, shall we?'

Staff Nurse Marsh gave a small tut of disapproval and Maisy couldn't quite decide whether this was because she thought that it was cheeky for a *patient* to answer a *doctor* like that or whether she was not particularly concerned about preserving the environment!

Matthew merely smiled. 'Indeed. I'm all for doing the planet a good turn!' He leaned back in his chair and stretched his long legs in front of him. 'So, tell me all about your difficulties conceiving a baby, Mrs Barnes.'

She blinked away some tears. 'You mean, tell you what I told my GP?'

Matthew nodded. 'If you don't mind. I always find it useful to hear the story firsthand.'

Mrs Barnes gulped, then shrugged. 'There's nothing to tell, really. We started trying about two years ago and since then—nothing.'

Matthew made a note on the piece of paper in front of him. 'And you've some preliminary investigations, I believe.'

Mrs Barnes ticked off her fingers as she recited, 'First I did my temperature charts to see if I was ovulating—'

'And?'

'I was. Regular as clockwork. So, next, Adam had his semen analysed, didn't you, Adam?'

Adam grew red around the ears, and Maisy's heart went out to him. The subject matter was making *her* feel embarrassed too!

'That's right,' mumbled Adam.

'And that was OK?' probed Matthew.

'More than OK,' said Mrs Barnes proudly. 'They said that he had *millions* of little swimmers!'

Matthew smiled. 'Excellent. Well, so far so good. What I'd like to do now, Mrs Barnes, is to a take a general medical history.'

'You mean, not just about my reproductive system?'

'That's exactly what I mean. Fertility can be affected by other systems in the body too, you know.' He twisted his gold fountain pen between long, tanned fingers. 'Any history of heart disease or diabetes in the family?'

'Nope.'

'And family history of difficulty in conceiving?'

Mrs Barnes shook her short, sensibly cut hair emphatically. 'Quite the opposite! Both sets of parents bred like rabbits! Adam's one of five and I'm one of four—and that doesn't exactly help!' she added impulsively. 'All our brothers and sisters keep asking when *we're* going to produce!'

Matthew nodded. 'Family and peer pressure often create the flashpoint which makes couples start investigating their failure to conceive. Any allergies?'

'Just to housework!'

He laughed. 'Bowels OK?'

'Couldn't be better—I eat a lot of lentils, Doctor!'

'Fine.' Matthew nodded. 'Are you on any medication just now?'

'I only ever treat myself homeopathically!' declared Mrs Barnes proudly.

Matthew scrawled something in the margin. 'Right. Have you ever had any operations?'

Mrs Barnes shrugged. 'N-no.'

'Didn't you say that you were in hospital for one of your birthdays? Years ago?' interjected Adam timidly.

Mrs Barnes screwed up her face in concentration. 'But that was just appendicitis.'

'Did they remove your appendix?' queried Matthew.

'Yes, they did. I remember being violently sick after the anaesthetic.'

Matthew scribbled something else. 'And when was that?'

'Oh, years and years ago—I was only a child.'

Matthew stopped writing. 'And was it a bad case? Can you remember?'

Mrs Barnes shook her head. 'Not really. All I can remember is missing Christmas *and* my birthday—which was in January—so I must have been in hospital quite a long time. And I was very hot—I remember that. And I had to take some ghastly tablets which made me feel even worse. Why are you so interested, Doctor? Is it relevant?'

Matthew turned to Maisy, who was watching his relaxed interviewing technique with fascination. 'Is it relevant, Dr Jackson?'

Maisy thought hard, then nodded. 'It could be. If it was particularly bad appendicitis—which went on to become peritonitis, for example—then it's possible that Mrs Barnes could have got a secondary infection of her Fallopian tubes from that.'

Mrs Barnes looked from Matthew to Maisy anxiously. 'And is that it, then, Doctor?'

Matthew raised his brows questioningly. 'How do you mean?'

'If that *is* the case does that mean I won't be able to have a baby? Ever?'

'Whoa, whoa, *whoa*!' Matthew sounded very like a cowboy gentling a horse. He held his hand up and somehow, rather magically, Maisy thought, managed to coax a smile from the woman sitting opposite him. 'Let's not jump the gun, shall we?' he said to her very kindly. 'The first thing we have to establish is whether or not your Fallopian tubes *have* been affected by what sounds very much to me like peritonitis.'

'And how will you do that, Doctor?' asked Mrs Barnes.

'By a simple procedure known as a laparoscopy and dye,' explained Matthew, and indicated that Mrs Barnes should lean over the desk and watch while he made a swift sketch of the abdomen.

'We make a tiny incision into the abdomen,' he said. 'See. Just here. And we visualise the area we want to look at. Then we inject a little radioactive dye, which will enable us to see whether the tubes have been damaged in any way or whether they are, in fact, perfectly patent.'

'And if they're not?' The male voice belonged to Adam, and they all turned to look at him.

'Then I would recommend you for IVF treatment,' said Matthew, 'provided, of course, that at least one of your ovaries hasn't been too damaged by scar tissue and is still able to produce eggs.' He wrote something else down on the notes before him, and then looked up at the couple. 'I'd like to examine you now, Mrs Barnes.' He indicated the couch, partially concealed by a screen at the far end of the room. 'So, if you'd like to go behind the screen with Staff Nurse Marsh and get undressed.'

Mrs Barnes smiled purposefully. 'Certainly, Doctor. Are you coming in, Adam?'

Adam blanched very slightly. 'Er, if you

don't mind, I'll sit here with the doctor.'

Maisy smiled at him reassuringly. She knew from past experience that some men baulked at the idea of watching their wives have an intimate examination—even men who appeared to be as trendy as Mr Barnes!

Staff Nurse Marsh bustled the patient in rather importantly, and Maisy noticed that Matthew diffused any anxiety in both husband and wife by giving a softly spoken running commentary from behind the curtain.

'Your abdomen is fine,' he said.

'Too fat!' came the reply.

'Nature's way of protecting the internal organs,' demurred Matthew jokingly.

'Thank you, Doctor!'

'And your uterus feels fine—no fibroids that I can feel on examination. Yep. That all seems perfectly satisfactory to me. OK, Mrs Barnes, you can get dressed now.'

He removed his gloves and washed his hands thoroughly, came and sat back down at the desk again and waited until Mrs Barnes had rejoined them.

'Now. . .' he smiled at both of them '. . .is there anything *you* would like to ask me?'

The patient shook her head. 'Not really. It's just. . .'

'Just what?' Matthew prompted, in a voice which made Maisy feel warm with admiration for him.

Because it was possibly the most understanding voice that Maisy could ever remember hearing a doctor using to a patient before, and it reinforced just what a sensitive subject the whole issue of fertility was. How remarkable, then, that the man who had rebuked her so thoroughly for her lateness could be capable of such compassion and understanding!

Fiddling with a silver pendant which hung from her neck, the patient screwed her face up. 'Just that, in a way, I almost hope that blocked tubes *are* the reason for my not having conceived so far—'

Maisy watched as Mrs Barnes stared at the consultant defiantly as if she expected him to look dramatically shocked, but he did no such thing. His expression remained resolutely approachable— and drop-down-dead gorgeous, Maisy thought grudgingly.

'Because it's easier to deal with a definite cause?' suggested Matthew. 'Rather than the unknown?'

'Exactly!' beamed Mrs Barnes after her initial look of astonishment—presumably at the fact that a remote hospital doctor could be so perceptive!

'Well, that's just human nature, isn't it?' suggested Matthew quietly. 'To want to know why.' He laid his pen down on the desk and looked up at Staff Nurse Marsh, who was gazing at him so dreamily that Maisy was filled with a sinking dread. Please don't let *my* face have been so transparent, she prayed silently. Let mine just have been looking at him with nothing more than a cool, professional detachment.

'Can you arrange a lap-dye as soon as possible please, Staff?' he asked.

'Certainly, Doctor,' said Staff Nurse Marsh, with

the kind of ecstatic smile she might have worn if he had just offered to make her Mrs Gallagher at the earliest opportunity!

'I don't know how to thank you!' said Mrs Barnes effusively, as she rose to her feet.

'I do!' said Adam immediately. 'By bringing a bouncing baby in to show you one day!'

'Well, that would be the dream scenario, yes,' admitted Matthew softly. 'But the most important thing to remember is that if you never do have a baby—and I'm afraid that the possibility must be considered—then there are many, many other ways of living a fulfilling life together. You have to try to live a normal life in the meantime. To get your desire to reproduce into perspective.'

He shrugged apologetically. 'I know it's easier said than done and I know that at the moment it's what you want more than anything else in the world, but having a child isn't *everything*, you know. And even if you do have a child you mustn't *make* that child everything. It's much too heavy a burden for him or her to carry. Do you understand what I'm saying?'

Mr and Mrs Barnes stared deeply into his eyes, as if shaken by his depth of perception. 'Yes, Doctor,' they answered eventually in thoughtful unison. 'And thank you for your honesty.'

'My pleasure,' answered Matthew, sounding as though he really meant it.

He looked up, and as Maisy found herself caught in the searchlight of his stare she felt as though someone had taken an invisible swipe at her. All the tiny, almost invisible hairs on the back of her neck began to tingle with an instinctive and unnerving reaction to that sweeping gaze. And not just that, either. Tiny beads of sweat had begun to prickle hotly around her hairline and her lips had gone oddly dry.

Had he noticed? she panicked silently. Was that why that small and unconsciously sexy smile had lifted the corners of his mouth?

Just in case he had, Maisy set her own mouth in the stubborn pout her brother and sisters would have laughingly commented on!

Concentrate, Maisy, she told herself sternly as she stared fixedly at his name badge. Just *concentrate*!

Fortunately, with the strength of character for which she was famous in the Jackson clan, she managed to do just that, focusing all her attention on the job rather than on the man sitting across the room from her.

For the rest of the afternoon a steady stream of couples marched through the door to see Matthew, while Maisy copiously made notes to draw her attention to points she didn't know and which she intended to look up in one of her textbooks that very evening.

Because she had a strong suspicion that Matthew Gallagher would expect immediate answers to any questions he shot at her. If today was anything to go by!

He didn't let her go until gone five-thirty, even though by that time she was pale and exhausted.

And there wasn't a flicker of emotion on his face

when eventually he glanced up and handed her three thick manila envelopes from his desk. 'Here are three research proposals for you to look over,' he said slowly. 'I want you to study them carefully and choose the one you find most interesting.'

'You're letting me *choose*?' she queried in surprise.

His raised his dark brows. 'Don't sound so surprised. I want you to do your very best research for me—and the way to guarantee that is to pick a subject about which you feel some passion. But you'll have to decide soon as the ethics committee is meeting next month and we need to get their approval first.' He registered her paper-pale face. 'You'd better go home now.'

Stiffly, taking the packages from him, Maisy got to her feet. 'Thanks.'

His eyes narrowed. 'Did you eat any lunch?'

'Yes,' she answered truthfully.

'But you're still very pale,' he commented thoughtfully.

There was something so relaxed and sympathetic about him that Maisy was terribly tempted to tell him all about the fact that her periods had been getting steadily heavier and more painful, but she resolutely resisted the temptation. 'That's my natural complexion,' she lied.

She had almost reached the door when she heard his deep voice.

'Just one more thing, Jackson—'

She turned around, and suddenly her fingers itched to slap a bit of make-up on her face. Or something. Her looks might have been somewhat unconventional but she certainly wasn't used to a man looking at her as though she were something the cat had dragged in!

She lifted her chin up, a movement which instinctively brought her lashes down to half shield her sooty-grey eyes, and the movement seemed to arrest him momentarily.

'Yes, Matthew?' she queried, in as haughty a tone as she could manage.

He smiled at the contrast between her fiercely proud expression and the wild, wild hair. 'You look as though you could do with a good night's sleep,' he told her candidly.

Maisy was outraged! First he was quizzing her on her dietary habits, and now this! 'Do you make personal remarks to *all* your juniors on their very first day?' she demanded indignantly.

'Not usually, no,' he admitted, his eyes glittering. 'But, then, my juniors don't usually turn up with their eyes shadowed from lack of sleep.'

Her eyes glittered back a defiant challenge of their own. 'Point taken, if somewhat overstated,' she answered back coolly.

'Just don't let it happen again,' he said curtly, and bent his head to begin to write.

Which Maisy took to be a rather rude gesture of dismissal!

CHAPTER FIVE

MAISY stamped out of Matthew's consulting room, resisting the temptation to slam the door and, instead, contenting herself with conjuring up images of Matthew Gallagher tripping up and falling headlong into a muddy ditch—or having a jug of cream tipped all over that shiny brown hair!

It was either that or give in to the infinitely more disturbing images which all seemed to involve kissing and touching and some very old-fashioned and masterful behaviour by her new boss. And especially disturbing to Maisy, who had been convinced by her ex-fiancé that she hadn't a sensual bone in her body.

So why was this peculiar hot and cold excitment currently fizzing its way up and down her nerve endings, leaving her a very confused person indeed?

Could a mobile and perfectly chiselled face and a pair of magnetic green eyes still have the power to seduce, even when the possessor of those attributes was the kind of arrogant, uncompromising man who clearly had a heart of stone?

But the moment Maisy left the clinic she walked straight outside into the invigoratingly salty blast of late afternoon sea breeze and it blasted some of the cobwebs away. She sniffed the air appreciatively, authoritative and attractive Australians momentarily banished from her thoughts.

She thought about what options lay ahead for her evening's entertainment. A pity, really, that Sarah was not around, Maisy thought with a small pang. She could have just called round and eaten supper with her and Jamie and Harriet and then come home and had an early night.

Although, on second thoughts, perhaps it was a bit of a blessing in disguise. For it wouldn't exactly encourage her to lead an independent life and to rebuild the self-confidence which Giles seemed to have single-mindedly set out to sabotage. Not if she was able to keep running around to her sister's and brother-in-law's house and using it as a safe haven every time she had a spare evening.

She yawned as she tucked the manila envelopes under her elbow and made her way back towards her room in the doctors' mess.

And, anyway, she ought to be sensible. After her frantic weekend she needed sleep badly, and she also needed to read up on all the various conditions she had come across today. As well as study Matthew's three research proposals at length.

And she still had to tackle her suitcases!

She decided to unpack first, then shower and eat an early supper in the mess. Afterwards she would curl up in bed with her textbooks and a bag of toffees!

And if that didn't sound like mature, adult behaviour Maisy no longer cared. And why should she care? she asked herself mutinously. She no longer had anyone to please, except herself, and nobody to answer to either.

To her everlasting regret, Maisy had spent the eight months of her ill-fated engagement to Giles trying to be exactly what he had wanted her to be. Someone who would always be prepared to fit in with exactly what *he* wanted to do. To express the kind of opinions *he* held so dear. And somewhere along the way she had left the real Maisy Jackson behind.

Well, maybe now the time was ripe to find her again. . .

Maisy walked into her room and looked around, her mind buzzing. It was perfectly true that at times she could have won a medal for chaotic living but old habits were hard to break, and with the ruthless efficiency she had had drummed into her at boarding school it took her less than half an hour to neatly unpack all her stuff and to stow the suitcases away.

At least the room now looked half-decent. And the view from her window was to die for—a broad slash of sapphire sea in the distance, with the green patchwork of the downs rising up behind it. With a couple of pictures covering up some of the bigger stains on the walls and a large jug of flowers brightening up that rather dreary mantelpiece, she would soon have the place looking like home!

She thought of all the wedding presents she and Giles had returned, and shuddered. All that delicate bone china with the discreet yet expensive gold edging. Middle-aged and middle-class! His choice, not hers. He had overridden her desire for Provençal pottery in rich, deep cobalt with splashes of saffron, pronouncing it too 'loud' for the kind of dinner parties he expected them to be giving.

How on earth had she landed up with a man who could hold such strong opinions on something as fundamentally unimportant as *pottery*? And how did she ever get to be such a yes-woman? Maisy found herself wondering in disgust.

She showered and washed her hair, knowing that if she didn't blow-dry it the natural kink would make it look like a wild, wheaten halo. But, frankly, she was too tired to do anything with it other than run her fingers through the silken waves and let it fall naturally to her shoulders. And, besides, Giles was no longer around to tell her that it looked much 'nicer' if it was blow-dried!

She pulled on a pair of her oldest jeans and put on a giant white cotton shirt which Ben had given her in one of his more benevolent moods, then set off towards the mess for supper.

It was always rather disconcerting to walk into a brand-new hospital canteen for the first time. Especially a hospital where you knew no one except one very grumpy Australian consultant and an equally unfriendly staff nurse!

But, to Maisy's relief, it was early and the place was empty save for one table which was occupied by two men in white coats, their faces smudged with tiredness. They had heaped plates of food before them, which they were attacking with the gusto and contemptuous disregard for calories which was nearly always associated with youth.

Housemen! thought Maisy immediately.

They looked up as Maisy walked in and one of

them, who had such a thick mop of hair that he
looked more like a rock star than a doctor, called
out, 'Hey! Doctor!'

Maisy smiled politely. 'Who? Me?'

'Yeah! You! Come and sit with us! Come on!'

Maisy shrugged. What the hell. She needed
friends right now! 'OK,' she agreed, and went over
to their table where she pulled out a chair and
sat down.

'We need the gentle charms of a woman to subdue
the animalistic tendencies of Ralph here,' said the
rock-star doctor, pointing to a pale man with an
intelligent, angled face and a brush of bright orange
hair which stood up on the top of his head. He
looked exactly like a fox, thought Maisy with
amusement, watching as he ate his way through a
gigantic portion of chocolate fudge cake and cream
with an expression of pure bliss on his face.

'Say hello, Ralph,' urged the rock-star doctor.

'Hello,' grinned Ralph as he looked up from his
chocolate cake.

'I'm Charlie Harris,' smiled the rock-star look-
alike. 'We're both on the surgical rotation for our
sins! First supper we've eaten together in almost
four months and we—'

At that moment the slim, black bleeper in Ralph's
pocket began shrilling with the relentlessness of a
singing kettle and the insistency of a crying new-
born, and he pulled an expressive face.

'Spoke too soon, didn't you, Charlie?' he sighed
with mock resignation, and rose to his feet as
the bleeping suddenly and surprising stopped. 'I'd

better answer it. Nice to meet you—?'

'Maisy.' She smiled very widely, slightly over-grateful because it was the first genuine welcome she had experienced since she had first set foot in wretched Southbury Hospital! 'Maisy Jackson. Pleased to meet you too!'

'And you,' said Ralph vaguely as the bleeper jangled into life once more, and he hurried towards the phone which hung on the wall beside the exit.

'Jackson?' mused Charlie, rubbing at his fashion-ably shadowed square chin with a thumb and forefinger. 'I'm sure I know the name Jackson.' He spread butter thickly all over a cream cracker and bit into it. 'Isn't there a gorgeous, green-eyed midwife—?'

'My sister,' put in Maisy hastily, in case he said something indiscreet or sexist. Or both!

'Ah!' Charlie exclaimed. '*Now* I have it!'

'You do?'

Charlie nodded. 'Uh-huh! She's the one who the much-admired Jamie Brennan wooed and married. And before anyone else had had the chance to even break bread with her! And now they're sickenly happy together, so I understand.'

'That's right,' beamed Maisy, her previous occasionally negative thoughts crumbling into dust for ever as her heart rejoiced that Sarah and Jamie had found each other. 'They are.'

'And is this the same Brennan. . .?' mused Charlie, one navy-blue eye narrowing with a mean-ingful glint, and Maisy found herself looking over her shoulder in alarm until she realised that he was winking at a particularly scrumptious-looking student nurse behind her! She hid a smile as she listened to what he was saying.

'The same Brennan,' continued Charlie, 'who took his beautiful bride and daughter off to the furthest flung reaches of the globe. . .to the *Antipodes*, no less!' he declared dramatically. 'And in so doing brought to these green and pleasant shores a surly Australian named Gallagher—'

'I don't know that I'd actually call him *surly*,' objected Maisy, who was scrupulously fair.

'You see!' complained Charlie, with a theatrical slap of palm to forehead. 'You've fallen into exactly the same trap as every other hot-blooded female below the age of ninety in this hospital—'

Maisy frowned. 'Which is what?'

'Of attributing to the man far more sex appeal than he actually possesses—'

'Says who?' butted in Maisy interestedly.

'Says me,' said Charlie immediately, turning his mouth down at the corners and managing to look thoroughly *sulky* into the bargain, thought Maisy, biting back a giggle.

'Don't know what they see in him,' he added disparagingly.

'Neither do I,' said Maisy, lying diplomatically.

'Although it isn't just the women in *this* hospital who behave like adolescent schoolgirls whenever he's around,' confided Charlie, quickly looking over both his shoulders as if the canteen was about to be raided by bandits! 'I happen to have a perfectly gorgeous friend—Becca—best doctor of her year, outrageously funny, heartbreakingly beautiful, and she. . .' His voice tailed off, leaving Maisy looking at him expectantly.

'She what?' prompted Maisy, who couldn't bear a half-finished story.

'She went to work in the same Sydney hospital as the devilish Dr Gallagher—in the same department, even! And there she ignored the advice of her Australian sisters who warned her that he was a no-good, two-timing rat—'

'Cut the clichés,' put in Maisy drily, 'and get on with the story!'

'She succumbed to the abundant charms of our arrogant Aussie,' said Charlie sadly. 'And now she's in trouble.'

There was something so shocking in the way that the young doctor uttered the damning phrase that Maisy felt her skin ice over.

He couldn't mean. . . He couldn't mean what she *thought* he meant. . . Surely? 'W-what do you mean, she's in trouble?' she queried breathlessly.

Charlie gave her a sharp look. 'She's pregnant, of course—what did you think I meant? *And* been deserted by the father—'

'The father being. . .?' Maisy held her breath.

Charlie frowned, as if she was being especially dense. 'Why, Matthew Gallagher, of course.'

'Are you sure?' she said quickly.

He frowned again. 'Of course I'm sure! It's strange, really, isn't it? All that progress women fought for and they can still end up with their careers stymied—and all for one little slip-up. . .' His voice was bitter as it tailed off, and then he seemed to pull himself together with an effort.

'Go and get yourself some food, Maisy,' he urged. 'Like Ralph, I can't promise to last the whole meal out, but while I have a few moments' rest from the tyranny of the bleeper you're very welcome to join me.'

But Maisy felt sick. And mostly because of the realisation of *why* she felt sick. She wasn't just shocked to hear of Matthew Gallagher's reputation, or the story of what had happened to Charlie's friend, Becca. She was bitterly *disappointed*. No, that wasn't right either. Disappointment was too mild a word for the feelings she was currently experiencing. Deep despondency was closer to the mark.

And *why* was she despondent?

Maisy sometimes found the truth painful, but that had never stopped her from confronting it before.

Because for all her posturing about Matthew Gallagher's arrogance and high-handedness there had been a part of her—a big part—which had admired his skill and intuitiveness as a doctor.

And if she was being *really* honest—and why not—because the part of her which had nothing to do with medicine or work or patients or sickness or cure—the essential female part of her which had everything to do with senses and feelings and dreams—*that* part of her had liked Matthew. Had liked him very much.

No. Like was the wrong word altogether. You

couldn't actually *like* someone if you didn't know them.

All right, then, she had been extremely and over-whelmingly attracted to him. In the sort of smack-in-the-mouth kind of way which had been nothing like the slow build-up of intimacy she had once thought existed between her and Giles.

Charlie sat looking at her questioningly.

She shook her head and silky wheaten curls shim-mered beneath the blinding white light of the overhead fluorescent strips. 'I'm not hungry,' she said truthfully, and then, seeing the confusion on his face, added, not quite so truthfully, 'I only came in here because I was looking for someone. But they're not here. Listen, I only arrived late last night and my room is in the most dreadful state—'

'Know the feeling,' said Charlie ruefully.

'So I'd better go.' Maisy's voice sounded genu-inely apologetic, and she meant it when she said, 'It was really nice to meet you.'

'Another time, perhaps?' smiled Charlie, with all the slickness of a good-looking man to whom chat-ting up women came as naturally as breathing.

'That would be lovely,' Maisy managed, though she thought that if she didn't get out of that cabbage-scented room in a minute she really *would* be sick.

'Oh, by the way,' said Charlie, just as she turned to leave, 'whose firm are you working on?'

'Didn't I tell you?' Maisy didn't dare turn to meet his eyes, but her profile remained expressionless. 'It's Dr Gallagher's, actually.'

As she clicked her way across the polished tiles

towards the exit she thought she heard Charlie say aloud to himself, 'Oh, dear! *Now* what have I done?'

But once outside again in the bracing sea air Maisy realised that she had compromised herself by telling Charlie that she wasn't hungry. She might have lost her appetite when hearing about Matthew Gallagher's caddish behaviour but the loss had been only momentary!

Maisy's appetite was legendary—especially since she was able to eat guargantuan meals without ever putting on an ounce! At home, as a child, she had always been called 'Hollow Legs'. And right now she was absolutely *starving*!

Her stomach gave a protesting rumble in perfect timing with her thoughts.

And as there was not a single item of food in her room how on earth did she intend feeding herself?

It took her less than a minute to decide. It was only seven-fifteen, for pity's sake! The night was young and the glory of one of England's finest cathedral towns beckoned. She would go into Southbury and find herself a decent meal!

It was a sunny evening, but Maisy was used to the vagaries of the British climate and so she quickly went back to her room and substituted a yellow, skinny-rib jumper for the overshirt she was wearing. It was both smarter and warmer, and for good measure she picked up her umbrella, too. Then she went to the reception area in the main building of the hospital, where she was informed that the hospital courtesy bus was just leaving for the city centre.

'And when is there a bus back?' asked Maisy.

The enthusiastic young receptionist shook her head regretfully. 'I'm afraid there isn't one. Not coming back. Not at night-time. This is the last one out, too, so you're lucky, Doctor.'

Lucky.

The word echoed round and round in Maisy's head as the bus slowly inched its way towards the ancient grey stone buildings of the city centre.

Was she?

She was young, free, fit and gainfully employed so very probably, in comparison with a great many people, then, yes, she *was* lucky.

So why, she asked herself as she alighted from the bus and stood still for a moment to get her bearings, was she feeling so pathetically gloomy?

Because of Matthew Gallagher? And finding out about his perfidy? His abandonment of a woman in trouble, which went against everything she believed in?

Maisy sighed as automatically she began to walk over the well-worn cobbled stones towards the cathedral itself. Sexual attraction was an infuriating thing because it was so indiscriminate, she decided. You didn't *choose* who you were going to fancy—you just *did*!

And although Maisy had railed against Matthew's arrogance and high-handedness that was hardly atypical behaviour from a hospital consultant, now was it? Quite a lot of male doctors strutted around the place, arrogantly thinking that they were God's gift to medicine and women and acting accordingly. Matthew was hardly breaking new ground *there*!

Because that was the reason she had reacted so strongly to him, of course it was. She fancied him. She fancied him like *mad*! It was quite an astonishing reaction for someone like Maisy, who had never experienced anything quite like it in all her twenty-seven years.

It had happened as instantly as an allergic reaction so perhaps she had better treat it in the same way as she would an allergic reaction—by avoiding all contact with the rogue subject wherever possible!

It was easy to stop thinking about him as the cathedral rose up in front of her, imposing and stately, its oyster-grey stones smooth and shiny from centuries of rain and wind and snow. A rock of ages, which had survived the steady onslaught of the elements. She hesitated by the massive west door just as the mighty clock began to chime eight times.

Maisy went to church on high days and holidays and that suited her just fine. But as she peered into the dark and dim interior of the vast church, shot with dazzling spears of light from the stained glass as it fell into muted rainbow pools on the well-worn tiles, she felt the oddest urge to go and seek solace in its calm.

Making her way down one of the shadowed side aisles, she sat down in one of the pews and had been there for about ten minutes when she heard a sound familiar to anyone who worked in a hospital. Someone was crying.

She glanced around, her attention drawn to a young woman who sat in one of the side pews with her head buried in her hands and her shoulders shaking silently with sobs.

The doctor and the woman in her made Maisy want to go over to offer some sort of support, but she didn't move. Instead, she quickly averted her eyes from the woman's obvious distress. Because, after all, churches offered anonymity and privacy, if that was what you wanted. And if you couldn't cry freely in church then where *could* you cry?

But just as she was thinking about leaving her eye was caught by a movement of the woman's head, which caused all her hair to shimmer down her back. It was particularly noticeable and beautiful hair—thick and curly and as black as the night, falling in a charcoal cloud to the woman's slender waist.

The woman looked up briefly as Maisy rose to leave, her grey eyes red from crying and her pale face all tear-stained, and Maisy was struck by a need to convey some kind of sympathy. She gave the woman a gentle smile, and the woman acknowledged the unspoken concern with a brief nod.

Outside again in the warm summer evening, with tourists thronging the streets and giving Southbury an almost carnival atmostphere, Maisy found exactly the kind of place in which she wanted to eat. An upmarket vegetarian restaurant where no one blinked an eye at her jeans, and where she was able to eat an enormous meal whilst kidding herself that it must be doing her good!

*   *   *

It was getting on for ten when she finally made her
way outside, but it was still light. She thought about
finding a taxi, but the memory of how much she
had just spent on her meal halted her. She was only
a doctor, for heaven's sake, and she was *supposed*
to be saving up for a mortgage!

The decision made, she found her way out
through the maze of narrow streets to where the
ugly sprawl of the modern city outskirts began, with
their jail-like multi-storey car parks, clogged-up ring
roads and utilitarian bus stops.

The grumbling queue was already large when she
joined it, and no bus came in the twenty minutes
that she stood there. Maisy, who wasn't averse to
waiting, was nonetheless irritated that she hadn't
had the foresight to bring something with her to
read. Time dragged when you had nothing to do!

The approaching hum of unleashed power was
enough to grab the attention of the bored assembly.

And the sight of a car more colourful and noisy
than the sedate family saloons which had been
steadily passing them was enough to bring the grumbling completely to a halt.

Even Maisy found her attention drawn to the cro-
cus-yellow sports car. But young men driving
fabulously expensive cars had a kind of universal
appeal about them, she reasoned, her heart rate picking up as the car drew closer and she realised that
the man driving it was actually aged about thirty—
and that she had spent the whole day with him.

Suddenly she felt ridiculously disadvantaged and
vulnerable, standing in a queue while he purred past

in his outrageously plush car, and she felt an overwhelming desire not to be noticed by him.

Hastily she dipped her head and began to study the white plimsolls on her feet, which were no longer as white as they used to be, and prayed that the driver wouldn't spot her. But as soon as she heard the sound of brakes being applied she knew that her wish had not been granted.

She closed her eyes briefly as she heard a short toot on the horn and a deeply distinctive Australian voice call out impatiently, 'Jackson!'

Every head in the bus queue swivelled round to look at her with interest and envy.

Maisy sighed. There was nothing for it but to turn round. She did, unprepared and slightly resentful that her heart should race like train when she finally allowed her eyes to rest on those gorgeous, moody-looking features.

'What?' she called back ungraciously.

Dark brows met in the centre of his forehead. Clearly he'd expected a more enthusiastic response than *that*! Should she have erected a welcoming banner in his honour? she wondered caustically.

'Are you going back to the hospital?' he drawled.

Deliberately Maisy allowed her gaze to travel to the sign by the stop on which huge letters stated, SOUTHBURY HOSPITAL. She raised her eyebrows. 'What do you think?'

'I don't think *you'd* like to hear what I think!' he answered darkly. 'Do you want a lift or not?'

'I will if you don't,' muttered a woman standing behind Maisy, and Matthew heard her and grinned

Biting back a desire to berate the woman for inflating Dr Gallagher's massive ego even further, Maisy walked to where he had parked the car and folded her arms across her chest. 'You're parked on double yellow lines,' she pointed out.

'Precisely!' he snapped as he twisted the key in the ignition. 'Are you getting in or not?'

Maisy hesitated. She had been about to say, 'No, thank you, I'd prefer to take the bus,' when she realised just how prim and pathetic this would sound.

His mouth twisted at her obvious reluctance. 'Make your mind up, will you?' he drawled, his sage-green eyes flickering over her in a way which seemed to have a direct effect on Maisy's ability to breathe. 'I'm not planning to entice you into the slave trade, you know. You want to get back to the hospital, don't you? Well, I'm offering to *take* you back to the hospital.' He made it sound as though he were explaining to a five-year-old the way to tie up her shoelaces. 'Aren't I?'

'Y-yes,' said Maisy doubtfully.

'Or did you imagine that I was going to take a very long detour in order to have my wicked way with you?' he mocked. 'Drive you out to some isolated beauty spot in order to start whispering sweet words of desire?'

[M]aisy went pink behind the ears. Although words [   ]—rather than desire—would have been *her* [   ] preference, hadn't he come perceptively [   ] [des]cribing one of her wilder fantasies about [   ] [cour]se I wasn't!' she retorted, and pulled the door open with much more force than she had intended.

He waited until she had shut the door—wincing very slightly as she slammed it—and snapped her seat belt on, before roaring off to the envy and admiration of most of the bus queue. 'Try not to wreck it,' he murmured drily.

'Why? Are you one of those men who's in love with his car?' challenged Maisy without thinking. 'The kind that. . .'

'The kind that what?' he prompted, but he hardly seemed to be listening, which made it seem much less like prying and more like a casual interest. 'Are we talking phallic substitutes here, Jackson?'

'No, we are *not*!' In the half-light Maisy blushed furiously. 'We're talking about the kind of man who puts his car second in the list of the most important things in his life,' she said, as she remembered the almost obscene care and attention which Giles had lavished on his E-type.

'Only second?' he queried with amusement.

'That's right.'

'The first being their woman?' he guessed.

'The first being their job,' corrected Maisy in a far more reasonable tone than the one she would have used if he hadn't said the word 'woman' in such a ridiculously elemental and gloriously goo-making way.

'I see,' commented Matthew Gallagher quietly, his narrowed eyes never leaving the road in front of him.

He was silent for several minutes, long enough

to lull Maisy into a false sense of security, before he said, 'So, who was he, Jackson?'

'It doesn't matter.'

'No,' he answered reflectively, 'it doesn't. Just rather fond of his car, I gather?'

He asked the question in such a matter-of-fact way that Maisy seemed to have no control over the words spilling out of her mouth. 'Oh, he devoted whole Sundays to it! Polishing the wretched thing as though the paintwork were the scented skin of a young girl! No seventy-year-old millionairess seeking eternal youth would have had more care lavished on her than that machine of his did!'

Some men massaged their egos, thought Maisy bitterly, some even their girlfriends. But not Giles. Oh, no! Giles had spent most of his spare time massaging the bodywork of his wretched car!

'Which doesn't actually tell me very much about the car,' mused Matthew, with a quirk at the corners of his mouth which came very close to being a smile, 'but rather a lot about your relationship with its owner.'

Maisy felt horrified. She clapped her hand over her mouth. 'Oh, hell!' she burst out. 'What must you think of me? I've never, *ever* spoken about Giles to anyone before. Not like that.'

'Who was Giles?'

'It doesn't matter.'

'Well, I rather think it does.'

Something in his tone made her say sulkily, 'Giles is my fiancé. Correction—my *ex*-fiancé.'

He glanced up into his mirror just as a motorbike

overtook them. 'So why do you feel so bad about expressing what sounds like a perfectly reasonable objection to the fact that your fiancé lavished all his attentions on his car? And not on you?'

'Because I shouldn't be telling *you*!' she cried out. 'You're—'

'I'm what?' he asked quietly.

'My boss,' she answered, equally quietly. 'And. . .' Again her voice tailed off. Words seemed suddenly *too* important with this man.

'And what? An outsider, too. An Australian. The man who is only here for six months, and too much of a stranger to understand other people's problems?' He gave a deprecating laugh. 'Is that it, Jackson?'

'No.' She shook her head, trying very hard not to show irritation when he called her 'Jackson' like that. 'I didn't mean it like that. I just feel disloyal, saying anything, that's all. Especially to a man whom I scarcely know—except in the purely professional sense, of course.'

'Is that an oblique kind of invitation?' he questioned silkily.

Maisy frowned. 'To what?'

'To get to know each other better?' He shot her a sardonic glance. 'Is this where I butt in to tell you that we could do something about it right now? Cue for me to slam my foot down on the brake and haul you passionately into my arms?'

It was an outrageous suggestion.

And a stupidly attractive one, too!

Maisy turned to look out of the window, buying

time to think up a suitably cool response. 'Yeah, sure, Matthew,' she agreed drawlingly. 'And that's the story of your life, no doubt!'

He gave an odd, bitter kind of laugh. 'Oh, that it were!'

She thought of what she had heard in the canteen, and steeled her heart against him. She looked out of the window at the speeding countryside.

He changed down a gear as he came off the dual carriageway by the huge sign for Southbury Hospital. 'You have family, don't you, Jackson?'

Maisy nodded. 'You know I do.'

'Not really. I know that your sister is married to Jamie Brennan, that's all.'

'Well, I have a huge family.'

'So why didn't you talk to *them* about the ex-fiancé?'

'Because. . .' Maisy shook her head so that the wheaten waves bobbed wildly. 'Oh, because my family is too big and too mad and too chaotic, I guess. They *mean* very well but they would all want to sit round the fire, discussing it. Discussing Giles. And the thought of that makes me shudder. I suppose I've just grown out of family conferences, but it seems that they haven't. I've changed, I guess.'

He nodded his dark head. 'Changes rarely happen simultaneously,' he observed slowly. 'That's something I've learnt about life. Some people push for it, others resist it—and it's perfectly natural and right to do either. Or neither,' he added, with a surprisingly heavy sigh. 'The status quo has a lot to be said for it.'

Maisy nodded, surprised at his perceptiveness and oddly reassured by it, too. And yet she wondered what had made him sigh like that... 'Of course, the other reason for not wanting to discuss it with them is far more selfish—'

'Oh? And what's that?' His almost restrained interest had a curiously uninhibiting effect on Maisy—she had seen him employ the same technique when he was interviewing patients.

She moved to rest her elbow against her seat so that her face was turned towards him. 'Just that if you have very nearly committed yourself to spending the rest of your life with a certain man, well...'

Her grey eyes looked very big in her pale, freckle-spattered face, thought Matthew suddenly. 'Well, what?' he said softly.

Maisy shrugged. 'If you then start complaining about him it not only seems like a betrayal of the person you once thought you loved but it also makes you wonder if you'll ever be able to trust your own judgement again where relationships are concerned—'

'You mean, after so nearly tying yourself down to someone who was clearly unsuitable for you all along?' he put in. 'If only you'd had the objectivity to recognise it?'

Maisy blinked in astonishment. 'That's *exactly* what I meant,' she said.

'Don't sound so surprised, Jackson,' he commented drily.

'But it was a very perceptive thing to say,' she pointed out slowly.

Matthew gave a smile that was more of a wince. 'Is it my gender or my race that makes you prejudge me, I wonder? The fact that I am a man or an Australian which excludes me from showing any degree of sensitivity or perception in your opinion?'

Maisy now felt hopelessly out of her depth. 'But that isn't what I said!' she protested.

'It's what you meant, though. Isn't it? I'm a man—therefore, you view me as the enemy.'

'I view you as the enemy because you were so rude to me in clinic this morning!' she lied.

'You were late.'

'So I was but, you have to admit, you over-reacted.'

He didn't answer for a moment or two, just moved into the slower lane to let some maniac with a death wish overtake him.

'Maybe I did,' he admitted, not wanting to analyse quite *why* she had aroused such a strong reaction in him. He shot her a glance. But, you know, you mustn't get burdened down with too much excess baggage. You aren't the first person in the history of the world to have had a relationship go wrong, you know, Jackson—'

'Gosh! You're not going to tell me that *you're* in the same boat, are you?' quizzed Maisy sardonically. Was he about to elaborate on the rather shocking piece of information that Charlie had told her about in the canteen earlier?

He smiled, but it was nothing deeper than an enigmatic curve of his lips. 'You're quite right, Jackson,' he said, as the car slid to a smooth halt

NO COST! NO OBLIGATION TO BUY!
NO PURCHASE NECESSARY!

PLAY "LUCKY 7"
AND GET AS MANY AS FIVE FREE GIFTS...

HOW TO PLAY:

1 With a coin, carefully scratch away the gold panel opposite. Then check the claim chart to see what we have for you – FREE BOOKS and gift – ALL YOURS! ALL FREE!

2 Send back this card and you'll receive specially selected Mills & Boon® Medical Romance™ novels. These books are yours to keep absolutely FREE.

3 There's no catch. You're under no obligation to buy anything. We charge nothing for your first shipment. And you don't have to make any minimum number of purchases – not even one!

4 The fact is thousands of readers enjoy receiving books by mail from the Reader Service™. They like the convenience of home delivery and they like getting the best new romance novels at least a month before they are available in the shops. And of course postage and packing is completely FREE!

5 We hope that after receiving your free books you'll want to remain a subscriber. But the choice is yours – to continue or cancel, any time at all! So why not take up our invitation, with no risk of any kind. You'll be glad you did!

You'll look like a million dollars when you wear this lovely necklace! Its cobra-link chain is a generous 18" long, and the beautiful puffed heart pendant will add the finishing touch to any outfit!

Play

"Lucky 7"

M7KI

Just scratch away the gold panel with a coin.
Then check below to see how many FREE GIFTS will be yours.

YES! I have scratched away the gold panel. Please send me all the gifts for which I qualify. I understand that I am under no obligation to purchase any books, as explained on the opposite page. I am over 18 years of age.

BLOCK CAPITALS PLEASE

MS/MRS/MISS/MR _____

ADDRESS _____

_____

POSTCODE _____

◄ DETACH AND POST CARD TODAY ▲

 WORTH FOUR FREE BOOKS
PLUS A PUFFED HEART NECKLACE

 WORTH FOUR FREE BOOKS

 WORTH THREE FREE BOOKS

 WORTH TWO FREE BOOKS

in the consultant's parking lot, 'I'm not. In fact, I'm not going to tell you anything. I rather think we've had enough True Confessions for one night, don't you?'

He reached over her and clicked open her door. He barely touched her. In fact, he *didn't* touch her, but he might as well have done for her body silently shrieked out a painful recognition of his proximity.

She didn't move but just sat there, dazed and confused. Here they were back at Southbury Hospital in what seemed like a nano-second. Time had flown alarmingly in the company of Matthew Gallagher.

'We're here,' he said, frowning slightly as he noticed her frozen position. 'Are you OK?'

Was she *OK*?

In that journey back to the hospital she had just unburdened her soul to him like some therapy junkie. And how was she going to feel about *that* first thing in the morning when she had to face him in the review clinic?

'Jackson?'

Matthew had leaned forward to stare at her and was clearly concerned, for his eyes were very soft in the moonlight.

And in that one moment Maisy made some kind of sense of that feeling she had been experiencing in his presence all day. As though she wanted him to pull her hungrily into his arms and never let her go. An illogical and yet unstoppable feeling. The French were always going on about it. Maisy furrowed her eyebrows. Now *what* was it called?

'Jackson?' he repeated quietly.

Through the mists of enchantment Maisy struggled to find words which wouldn't condemn her to the same fate as many others—for surely he had had hundreds of star-struck women in his car before tonight? Women who had sat like this, unable to move, scarcely able to breathe.

Her breath caught in her throat as she realised that those intriguing eyes were far closer than they would have been under normal circumstances.

And suddenly these were not normal circumstances. For Maisy stared back at him, and in that brief, intense moment when their gazes locked—and fused—something happened. Something which seemed to make the air sing around them.

She held her breath.

Matthew frowned, compelled by an instinct he did not entirely trust, let alone begin to understand. His actions seemed to be beyond the control of his will as he leant forward to kiss her swiftly and very sweetly on the lips.

As kisses went it was remarkably innocent and it lasted no more than a few seconds, yet Maisy felt as breathless as if she had just run a race. She had never been kissed with quite so much tenderness before.

With Giles, even in the early days, a kiss had always been a hard, almost brutal expression of male domination—a declaration of sexual intent and nothing more.

'Wh-what did you do that for?' she whispered stupidly.

He smiled, but it was an odd, curving and some-what regretful smile. 'Because the moment was right. Because I was curious. Because I wanted to—and so did you.'

Yes.

'But it was a kiss,' he mocked laconically. 'Just a kiss, and nothing more.'

And then very gently he leaned across her to push the door of the car open. 'Goodnight, Jackson,' he murmured softly. 'Don't worry about it.'

Worry about what? About unburdening herself to him? Or about the effect his lips had had on hers? Somehow she turned to face him. She even smiled. Pulled a floppy, wheaten curl off her mouth and said, 'You're absolutely right, of course. After all, what's in a kiss? Goodnight, Matthew. And thank you for the lift home. I'll see you in the morning.'

His eyes were teasing now. 'Early start, don't forget.'

'I won't.'

Keen to get as far away from him as possible, Maisy strode briskly across the forecourt where her attention was suddenly caught by the figure of a woman walking ahead of her, her head bent low, as if deep in thought, her shoulders hunched and tense.

It was her strained stature as much as the free-flowing ebony waves of her remarkable black hair which made Maisy realise that this was the woman she had seen sobbing so disconsolately in the cathedral. Now what was she doing *here*? she won-dered. And what connection did she have with Southbury Hospital? She watched as the woman turned off purposefully in the direction of the nurses' home. A nurse, perhaps?

Matthew sat motionless in the car, his gaze following Maisy as she walked towards the doctors' mess, waiting until the last flick of her shadow disappeared.

Then and only then did he shift his long frame from the car. Locking the door behind him, he set off in the same direction as his new registrar—his eyes narrowed, his face lost in thought.

CHAPTER SIX

To Maisy's abiding surprise and pleasure, she fell into a deep and dreamless sleep as soon as her head hit the pillow, and the following morning she was bounding around her room full of energy and enthusiasm.

And determined to see take what had happened last night for what it was. A quick kiss between a man and a woman, nothing more—and certainly not a sensual act which had rocked the foundations of her world!

And which, she tried to convince herself, had absolutely nothing to do with the fact that this morning she spent much longer than usual checking her appearance!

Yesterday she had been so rushed that she had been at a definite disadvantage—especially when confronted by the attractive but distinctly unfriendly Samantha Marsh. Today she intended to show the unit that she did not *always* resemble a scarecrow who was badly in need of a make-over!

She did nothing more dramatic than apply the merest lick of make-up, but she tamed the flaxen halo of her hair with two tortoise shell clips and wore one of her favourite shift dresses. It was a bright, buttercup yellow, made from a mixture of linen and silk, and while most of it didn't actually *show* as long as she had her white coat on the scooped neckline was very flattering beneath the severe and mannish lapels of her doctor's uniform.

She added a string of amber beads and a matching pair of silver and amber earrings, which had been a birthday present from her brother and his wife, and stood back to survey herself in the mirror, pleased with the result.

Then, seeing that she had plenty of time before she was due in the clinic, she went down to the canteen, where she sat with a red-eyed Charlie who regaled her with detailed and gory stories of his surgical admissions throughout the night.

But Maisy had been surrounded by medicine all her life—and certainly long enough to be immune to distressing tales. Charlie's blood-curdling stories did not spoil her appetite in the slightest!

She calmly ate a poached egg and wholemeal toast and drank gallons of good, strong black coffee, her equanimity shattered only by the sight of Matthew Gallagher joining the queue at the counter.

'Isn't there a special dining-room for consultants?' Maisy hissed, when she was sure that there was no chance of her boss hearing her.

Charlie followed the direction of her gaze and his mouth twisted as he watched the tall, dark consultant reach out and take a dish of fresh fruit. 'Sure there is,' he said with a scowl. 'But our super-dooper Aussie doesn't agree with what I understand he calls "segregated socialisation". Consequently, he eats wherever takes his fancy—although I suspect it depends on *who*ever takes his fancy! He eats with the nurses sometimes. Quite a lot, in fact.'

Maisy found herself smiling as she dabbed at her mouth with her napkin and rose to her feet, determined to beat Matthew into work this morning. She rather liked the sound of a senior doctor who ate with the nurses, even if the pathetic, slightly smitten side of her found herself experiencing a pang of jealousy. After all, two of her sisters and her beloved sister-in-law were nurses, and they were always complaining about being treated like second-class citizens by the medical staff!

Maisy took her tray with her and stacked it neatly on the pile. She tried her best not to act self-consciously but it wasn't easy, not with Matthew sitting there calmly eating his breakfast. Had he seen her? she wondered. And was he remembering and regretting now that brief but rather beautiful kiss?

Matthew didn't notice her until she was almost at the door, and when he did he was astonished to find himself studying her surreptitiously while absent-mindedly taking much too large a mouthful of coffee and scalding the inside of his mouth in the process.

Had she seen him? And, if so, was she ignoring him because she was embarrassed about last night? Because she simply wanted to forget all about it?

Oh, for heaven's sake, man! Matthew thought to himself impatiently. Since when did you start to over-analyse such a perfunctory kiss?

Since last night, it seemed, he decided reluctantly, a wry smile curving his mouth into such a devastating smile that a student nurse carrying a loaded tray stood stock-still and just stared at him, momentarily arrested by such stunning good looks.

But Matthew's attention was elsewhere.

Magnetic in a sunny yellow dress whose vibrant colour seemed to be reflected in her glossy curls, Matthew found himself studying Maisy obsessively.

Just what *was* it about her that drew his eye to her so compellingly? he found himself asking. Because he had already decided that Dr Maisy Jackson was the antithesis of what he liked in a woman.

True, she was tall and slim, with a fit-looking body whose natural, firm curves seemed to have a lot more to do with healthy living than the excessive dieting which infuriated and bored him. And that pale, freckle-spattered skin, teamed with such thick, honey-coloured hair, was certainly very unusual.

But she was too. . .too. . .

Their eyes met briefly and Matthew scowled and slammed his cup down in his saucer. There was something about her which made his hackles rise. Something disturbing in those slate-grey eyes. Intelligent, perceptive eyes. Truthful eyes.

Matthew had grown up in a house surrounded by beautiful but scheming women. Women who had used their femininity quite ruthlessly towards their own ends. Consequently, in adult life he had been drawn automatically towards manipulative women, something which he had grown to profoundly regret.

And yet he suspected that Maisy Jackson did not have a manipulative bone in her body.

So why did that one innocent supposition

about her frighten the life out of him?

He watched the way her hips moved beneath her white coat as she disappeared out through the plastic swing doors. Then he smothered a croissant with cherry jam and bit into it unenthusiastically.

Maisy went straight into the main reception of the assisted conception clinic, to find Samantha Mason fiddling around with a glass bowl of flowers which decorated the counter of the large desk. She must have heard Maisy approaching but she didn't bother to look up, just continued to adjust a spray of small white roses unnecessarily.

As she did so some of the petals began to fall on the polished surface of the wood, and she made a small sound of annoyance as she plucked them up between her fingers. She glanced up then, unable to ignore Maisy any longer.

Maisy had already decided that she would be as pleasant as possible to the rather prickly staff nurse. 'Good morning, Staff Nurse,' she said sunnily. 'What beautiful flowers!'

Samantha looked momentarily disconcerted. 'Er—thanks,' she stumbled. 'I do them myself every day.'

'Thank heavens for that—I only have to *look* at a flower and it wilts immediately! My father always tells me that whatever the opposite of green fingers is I've got it!' Maisy pulled a notebook out of her pocket and leafed through it. 'Now, let's see. It's the review clinic first thing, isn't it?'

'Spot on, Jackson,' came a familiar mocking voice behind her.

Beneath her white coat Maisy felt her skin prickle with excitement. She turned around to face him, carefully composing her face into the neutral and keen expression of a junior doctor, determined that she would not present him with the breathless and eager air of a woman who rather wanted to be kissed again! Even if she did!

'Good morning, Dr Gallagher,' she said formally.

'I thought we'd agreed that you would call me Matthew,' he reminded her, and the green eyes sparked with something which closely resembled humour. 'But only when there are no patients around, of course.'

'Oh, of course,' agreed Maisy, laughing.

'Are the notes for the review clinic in my office, Samantha?' he asked.

'Everything has been ready for you since half past seven, Matthew,' answered Samantha rather grimly. 'As usual.'

'Thanks very much,' he smiled. 'Ready, Jackson?'

'Lead me there,' said Maisy, but she felt almost sorry for the staff nurse for there was no disguising her pained expression when she heard him address Maisy so familiarly.

Privately she wondered whether Matthew wasn't slightly overdoing it on the camaraderie front. But maybe his little nickname for her had a hidden agenda. Was the staff nurse's puppy-like enthusiasm where her boss was concerned a minor irritation to him? And was Matthew using a coward's way of telling Samantha that he simply was not interested in her romantically?

Banishing her thoughts as pointless conjecture, Maisy followed Matthew into his office, where he sat down behind the desk and motioned for her to take the chair beside him.

A blue jar of vividly coloured anemones stood on the desk. The office was bright and golden with the morning sunshine and he seemed totally at ease with himself—and with her. Not a bit concerned about late-night lifts and kisses, she thought, and suddenly Maisy felt filled with excitement at the prospect of working with a man who was the acknowledged expert in his field.

He pulled a referral letter towards him, scanned it and then looked up. 'So, who comes to see us at a review clinic?' he quizzed.

'Basically, couples who have been through treatment for infertility and have failed,' said Maisy immediately.

He nodded thoughtfully. 'Let's put it another way, shall we? Why don't we say patients whose treatment has been unsuccessful so far? I dislike the use of the word failure when it is associated with medical treatment over which the patient has very little control. Can you see that?'

'Sorry,' said Maisy, chastened.

But he shook his head. 'No, don't apologise. That was not an admonishment, Jackson, more a lesson in the appropriate use of language. This is supposed to be a learning experience for you. Right?'

'Right,' she answered with a wide smile.

The pure trust in that beaming wattage of a smile was a subtle warning to Matthew. He remembered how easily she had confided in him last night and knew how easily such an unburdening of the heart might make a vulnerable woman like Maisy Jackson emotionally dependent on an impartial hearer.

And of her vulnerability he had no doubt. He could see it in those clear and strangely innocent grey eyes. There must be no emotional dependence. He must not let that happen. Not in this case. He must be boss and tutor to her and no more. Anything more would be dangerous to them both.

Fixing her with his most professional expression, he said, 'Then let's get Mr and Mrs Williams in, shall we?'

Maisy stood up, unable to shake off a vague feeling of disappointment and acutely aware that some precarious balance in the relationship between them seemed to have shifted and altered. 'Certainly,' she answered, echoing his own cool tone.

Mr and Mrs Williams were a couple in their late thirties, both smartly dressed for the office. Mrs Williams had sleek, dark red hair which hung in an glossy bell to brush the shoulders of her immaculate grey suit, and she wore high heels which should have carried a health warning. Maisy saw her sneaking a glance at her wristwatch as the couple took their appointed places opposite Matthew.

Matthew clearly noticed it, too, for he remarked, 'You're on a tight schedule?'

Ignoring her husband's frown, Mrs Williams

nodded vigorously. 'I'm afraid we are, Doctor. I'm due at a meeting in the centre of Southbury at ten-thirty so we'd better press straight on.'

Matthew nodded and, leaning back in his chair, thoughtfully surveyed the attractive woman opposite him before he spoke. 'Dr Jackson is my new registrar and is going to be doing some research during her year here. However, this is the first time she has actually worked in a unit like ours and so I may ask you to explain your treatment to her. How it affected you, and so on. For there is no more valuable learning tool, in my opinion, than in hearing experience firsthand. You have no objection to that, I trust?'

Mrs Williams gave an uncertain smile and another surreptitious glance at her watch. 'As long as it won't hold me up.'

'It won't make the slightest difference to your time,' said Matthew wryly. He looked down at the notes in front of him, before taking a deep breath. 'Unfortunately, your first two attempts at IVF have been unsuccessful,' he observed in a tone which Maisy for the life of her couldn't decipher.

'Unfortunately, yes,' answered the woman briskly, sweeping a stray strand of glossy red hair behind one perfectly shaped shell-like ear.

Matthew read through the notes. 'The first time it seems that you had a poor response to ovarian stimulation—'

'Too right I did!' the woman exclaimed heatedly. 'And it's hardly surprising! It seems to me that who-ever designed the regime had absolutely no idea that today's woman happens to be a *busy* woman!'

'Perhaps you'd just like to tell Dr Jackson about the regime,' suggested Matthew.

Mrs Williams gave Maisy a conspiratorial glance as she turned her eyes heavenwards. 'It started with the nasal spray—I had Nafarelin—one sniff in each nostil from day twenty-one of my cycle—'

'To stop natural ovarian activity.' Maisy nodded. 'Any side-effects?'

'You can say that again! I couldn't sleep, I had hot flushes and, what's more, I was jolly irritable—'

'No more than usual!' said her husband mildly, and was rewarded with a glare.

'The treatment, of course, induces a temporary menopausal state,' observed Matthew, 'but these side-effects were explained to you fully before you started the treatment?'

Mrs Williams nodded. 'Oh, yes. And I was fully prepared for them—or so I thought.'

'Easier in theory than in practice, perhaps?' suggested Matthew quietly.

Mrs Williams nodded. 'It certainly was. I had a rush job at work that week, and having to keep having daily injections of hormone *and* still keep sniffing that wretched spray quite wore me out. And then there were all the ultrasound scans that I had to fit in to see the response of the ovaries. Something had to give.'

'It did,' agreed Matthew calmly. 'And work won out in the end.'

Mrs Williams gave him an incredulous look. 'I *beg* your pardon?'

Matthew remained unperturbed by her hostility.

'It's written here in the notes that your Nafarelin regime was somewhat patchy—to say the least. You told one of the nurses that you had missed quite a few doses of your nasal sprays.' He looked at the patient questioningly.

'Only a few!' blustered the woman defensively. 'I don't think that people realise just how *busy* my life is! Anyway, the second time around I took the wretched stuff as regular as clockwork—John made sure of that,' she added, with a dark look at her husband which implied that he had nagged her into it!

'Indeed you did,' agreed Matthew pleasantly. 'And the conditions for IVF were fine.' He paused. 'But, unfortunately, you turned up late for your progesterone injection—'

'Only by a couple of hours—'

'Mrs Williams,' said Matthew slowly, 'I cannot emphasise enough how *crucial* the timing is. The progesterone injection which matures the eggs in the follicles must be timed for thirty-four to thirty-six hours before going to Theatre for egg collection. Failure to fall within that time-scale can render the whole operation futile. Consequently, we were unable to proceed—and all your sniffing and scans were to no avail.'

Mrs Williams crossed her arms across her chest. 'I had a client meeting I couldn't miss,' she told him stubbornly. 'My job is very important to me, Dr Gallagher.'

'I don't doubt that for a moment,' commented Matthew, 'but I think that at this stage in the proceedings we have to address a few fundamental issues.'

'Like what?' she demanded. 'I can have another go, can't I? You give people three goes here. I know that—two of my friends have been patients of this unit. So what's the problem?'

Maisy watched Matthew with interest, wondering just how he would respond to the woman's rudeness. She knew that some doctors, particularly those who had reached the dizzy heights of consultancy, simply would not tolerate being spoken to like that by a patient.

And yet, to her surprise, Matthew's expression showed no distaste or anger or censure. Indeed, he looked remarkably unperturbed.

He realigned his gold and black fountain pen so that it lay straight in front of him, before looking back up at the patient who sat with a mulish expression in front of him. 'You had counselling before starting this course of treatment, didn't you?' he said.

Mrs Williams stared at him. 'You know I did.'

He nodded. 'And obviously you and your husband will have talked through with the counsellor the effect of this kind of treatment on your life and on your relationship. How undergoing IVF is not simply a case of having a fertilised egg implanted into your uterus; that all the various procedures which go hand in hand with IVF can be very demanding, both mentally *and* physically. As well as very time-consuming,' he finished, a question in his eyes.

'You can say that again!' Mrs Williams responded predictably. 'There's an absolute fortune waiting to be made for the first obstetrician who can invent a single-dose treatment—so why don't you do your research on that, Doctor?' she finished, looking directly at Maisy.

Maisy knew that it was supposed to be a joke and, indeed, Mrs Williams looked at each of them expectantly. But nobody laughed.

Matthew gave a small sigh. 'I think that before we go any further down this particular road you have to ask yourself whether your desire for a baby is less or more important than your job.'

Mrs Williams sat bolt upright. 'Are you refusing to treat me, Doctor?' she demanded icily. 'I *do* happen to be paying for the privilege, after all. And that makes it business. And therefore in this case, as in the rest of the world of business, whether or not I happen to miss a few snorts of some drug is down to me.' She fixed him with another challenging and, frankly, hostile stare.

But again Matthew did not rise to it. His face was a picture of calm, thought Maisy, her admiration for his sang-froid mixed with indignation that his patient had had the nerve to speak to him in such a way!

'That isn't the way we work in this clinic,' he responded in a quietly stoical voice. 'We have hundreds of women clamouring for treatment, women who have saved and saved for the chance to have a baby. Women who are worried about the inevitable march of time—who know that with every year that passes their fertility is on the decline. Women, moreover, whose fiancial situation does not give them the luxurious option of repeated attempts.'

'And what has that got to do with *me*?' Mrs Williams demanded, a pulse ticking angrily in one smooth pale cheek.

Her husband spoke for the first time. 'Everything,' he answered in a tight voice, whose very control made it sound all the more dangerous. 'The doctor is saying that there are only so many people you can treat. That if you keep giving time to patients who aren't properly committed then it's a waste of treatment that they could have given to someone who *is* committed.' He drew a deep, accusing breath. 'You also told the doctor that you attended counselling—well, that's a laugh!'

'John!'

'No! Let *me* talk for a minute,' he interrupted angrily. 'I've had to sit here and listen to *you* for long enough!'

Maisy threw Matthew a questioning stare. Was he going to allow marital disharmony to degenerate into a full-scale war, here in his office? she wondered. But a barely perceptible shake of his head in her direction was enough to make Maisy continue to sit quietly with her hands folded in her lap, her entire attention now on the couple in front of her.

Mr Williams rounded on his wife. 'When we went there you didn't take a blind bit of notice of what the counsellor was saying!' he accused.

'I did! I did! I said—'

'You said exactly what you thought she wanted

to hear!' he returned cuttingly. 'You'd read enough textbooks and spoken to enough people to know just the right approach to take to have the counsellor believing that you were dedicated to the treatment. You manipulated her, Glenda, the same way that you manipulate everyone!'

At this point Matthew intervened. 'I think perhaps that Dr Jackson and I should let you talk this over in private—'

'No!' Mr Williams shook his head spiritedly. 'Stay!'

'Yes, stay!' grated Glenda Williams. 'You're the one who started all this!'

Maisy noted the narrowing of Matthew's sage-green eyes, but that tiny movement was the only indication that he was annoyed.

'Please stay,' Mr Williams appealed. 'If you go she'll turn the tears on—she always does. And then I'll find myself agreeing with everything she says, just as I always do, and we'll be back on the same old roundabout.'

'What do you want from me, John?' asked his wife shakily. 'A child at all costs? Am I just a womb to you with no life of my own? Is that it? Is that what you want?'

'I want *honesty* from you!' he breathed vehemently. 'Nothing more or less than that! If you genuinely don't want a baby—if your career is too important for you to want to give it up—then *tell* me, and we can discuss it. But, for God's sake, let's stop going through with this whole farce of not doing the treatment properly, so that it's neither one thing nor the other. It's a waste of the unit's time and your time and my time, and it's a waste of money! More importantly, it's a waste of all the emotional energy we expend when we enter into something like this.'

There was complete silence in the room and then a small shaky voice said, 'But I did it for *you*, John.'

'You shouldn't do it just for me,' he said gently. 'You should be doing it for yourself too.'

'I thought you wanted a baby more than anything else in the world!' she cried.

'Only if that's what you want too,' he said softly. 'We have to be in total accord over something as important as having a baby. I *do* happen to be aware of how important your career is to you. Marriage is supposed to be a partnership, you know.'

'Oh, John!' she wailed, and burst into tears.

Matthew leaned over and provided the tissues while Maisy went out of the office to rustle up a tray of coffee.

By the time she returned everything seemed to have calmed down. Mrs Williams sat, red-eyed, clutching her husband's hand like a teenager on a first date.

She looked up as Maisy walked in and took the coffee from her gratefully. 'I wanted to be a success in my career, you see,' she said, unprompted.

'And you are,' commented her husband. 'But you're in danger of wearing yourself into the ground.'

'I thought I could have it all! The baby *and* the career!'

'Lots of women do,' said Matthew, taking his coffee from Maisy, and she could have sworn that he winked at her. 'But there have to be changes. You can't carry on working all the hours that God sends *and* have a baby—and no one is saying that when you have a baby you must never work again. You just need to compromise—to juggle your commitments effectively. There's no need to spread yourself so thinly on the ground.'

Maisy was fascinated by his words. What a wonderful husband and father he would make, she found herself thinking, before drawing herself up in horror.

She had just escaped from the confines of an ill-fated engagement which should have been enough to put her off marriage for ever, and yet here she was, contemplating marriage to a man who was little more than a stranger to her!

Mrs Williams nodded, obviously as impressed now with Matthew's words as Maisy was. She drank some of her coffee, then looked up at the consultant anxiously. 'You *will* let us go ahead with the third treatment, won't you, Dr Gallagher?

'I wouldn't dream of being so authoritarian as to forbid you from making another attempt,' he told her, 'but I think that what you need right now is a little rest and recuperation. You've been under a lot of stress with work and with the treatment. I think you need to go away with your husband and to spend some time talking. Decide what your priorities are. About what decisions you need to make.

'Let's see.' He glanced down at the notes again.

'You're thirty-one at the moment. If the job needs one hundred per cent commitment right now, there is still time to have a baby—either when those demands have lessened or when they no longer seem quite so important to you. Then you can come back and try again—if that's what you both want.' He smiled. 'Just don't leave it too long.'

'The biological clock,' said John Williams, echoing all their unspoken thoughts.

'That's right,' said Maisy softly. 'Some women regret that they never heeded its ticking.'

Matthew glanced up at her with narrowed eyes and gave a brief nod, as though he agreed whole-heartedly with her sentiment, and Maisy felt disproportionately pleased to have his approval for once!

The couple stood up at last to leave. Mrs Williams blew her nose. Her eyes and nose were red, her cheeks were blotchy and the immaculate red hair was ruffled.

Funny really, thought Maisy, how much more *human* she looked than the sleek, hard woman who had walked into the consulting room! But that was what expressing emotion did for you, she decided. You may not always like it but it certainly was a great leveller!

'Thank you, Dr Gallagher,' said Mrs Williams, shaking the tall obstetrician's hand. 'Isn't human nature odd? I always thought that John thought of my career as dispensable, and now that he has been so reasonable about it I suddenly find that I feel overwhelmingly broody!'

They all laughed.

'Let's go,' said John, taking her hand.

'Do I look frightful?' she quizzed anxiously.

You look gorgeous,' he told her, and kissed the tip of her nose with a tenderness that made Maisy smile at them indulgently but, then, she was rather sensitive to tender kisses herself at the moment. She just hoped that Matthew hadn't noticed!

They sat in silence for a few moments after the door had closed behind the couple.

Maisy felt rather than saw Matthew studying her. And when she looked into that dazzling green gaze she found that his expression was questioning, as if he cared what she thought about the consultation. 'She was pretty rude to you,' she commented. 'Didn't you mind?'

He shrugged. 'She was emotional. It's an emotional subject. It's par for the course with this job.'

Maisy smiled. 'Are you always so reasonable?'

He gave a laugh. 'Oh, it's easy enough to be reasonable when you're wearing a white coat and sitting behind a desk and dealing with a subject about which you know a great deal. I can be as unreasonable as the next person!'

'Do you think they'll come back?'

He was silent for a moment. 'If they do she'll put all the passion and commitment she currently puts into her work into the treatment. And, yes, I think they will come back—and probably sooner than they imagine.'

'So, did their counselling fail?' asked Maisy. 'Shouldn't all those ambivalent feelings have come out before—I mean, before they had gone so far down the line?'

'Of course they should,' answered Matthew. 'But counselling isn't a skill, like piling bricks up on top of one another. When you are dealing with fragile emotions and doubts and uncertainties slip-ups are bound to happen occasionally. And, as Mr Williams said, she told the counsellor exactly what she wanted to hear. I must tell Lucie about it.'

'Lucie?'

'Our counsellor. I'll introduce you.'

'But won't she be upset? Won't she see it as a kind of criticism?'

He smiled. 'Oh, no. She's astute and she has a remarkable degree of insight. Knowing Lucie, she'll look on it as a learning experience of her own.' He looked down at his notes. 'Only two sets of patients left. Like to call them in?'

'Sure.' Maisy rose noiselessly to her feet.

She was almost at the door when he said, in quite a different voice, 'Jackson?'

She smiled again, unable to stop herself. In spite of his less-than-flattering nickname for her! After less than two days of working with him she was discovering that she really *liked* him. 'Uh-huh?'

'Where do you happen to stand on the subject of career versus babies?'

She paused to think about it for a moment, then lifted a clenched fist to her mouth, as if speaking into an imaginary microphone in the perfectly modulated tones of the professional newsreader. Not for nothing had she been known as the best mimic during the annual charades the Jackson family used to play every Christmas! 'I believe that it *is* possible to combine the two roles successfully—depending, of course, on the co-operation of both partners.'

'And what if it's a single mother?'

Maisy tipped her head to one side and considered. 'Much more difficult,' she continued, still in the same quasi-professional voice. 'Obviously, some women are forced to be lone parents through circumstance, but I have to say that it is not a situation that I would ever be in through choice.'

He bit back a smile. She really was very good at sounding exactly like one of those bland women who often fronted current affairs programmes on television! And she didn't seem to take herself too seriously either. During his illustrious and fairly charmed life, Matthew had met very few women like that.

Maisy probed for some kind of reaction to her remarks. 'Though you probably think that's terribly old-fashioned of me?'

He shook his head, golden and burnished in the sunlight. 'Not at all. I believe that a happy and settled partnership is the ideal and preferable framework for bringing children into the world.'

Maisy's eyes widened happily. 'What awful conformists we sound, don't we?'

He wasn't sure that he agreed with *that* particular sentiment, although right now—with her wheaten mop of hair looking like glossy curls of butter, and her shining grey eyes and her infectious smile—he seemed unable to think up a suitable reply which he would not greatly regret later.

His track record with women would do no favours to a woman like Maisy Jackson, who was still recovering from a broken engagement—although, admittedly, to a man whom she sounded well rid of.

Nevertheless. . .

Resisting an extremely strong temptation to ask her out for a drink after work that evening, Matthew forced himself to adopt the kind of tone which would kill the conversation stone dead. 'Perhaps you'd like to call the next set of patients in now?'

And Maisy, suddenly aware of something forbidden in his voice and not knowing what had caused it, swallowed a feeling of disappointment as she replied, 'Certainly, Matthew.'

CHAPTER SEVEN

MAISY spent the next few weeks familiarising herself with Southbury Hospital and the assisted
conception clinic, and quickly learnt that Matthew
expected nothing less than one hundred per cent
dedication from her!

But she didn't mind that. She had never had a
problem with work, however hard, it was just
relationships which had so far proved to be her
downfall!

She settled into the routine easily enough, and
soon felt as though she had worked there for ever.
Soon she knew without having to stop and think
about it that they did egg collections twice a week,
ultrasound scanning every morning and embryo
transfers twice a week. Added to that there were all
the treatment planning sessions and review clinics to
fit in, as well as twice-weekly counselling sessions.

She also discovered that all these different treatments generated a great deal of paperwork, and that
it was best to deal with it immediately if you didn't
want a hefty backlog to cope with when you were
supposed to be off duty.

And, surprisingly, Matthew took it on himself to
be her guide. He took her to all the related units
in the main part of the hospital and introduced
her to their various consultants. She particularly

liked Alan Parker, who was one of the obstetricians and gynaecologists, and she also met the paediatric consultant—an enchanting man with an enchanting name.

'This is Leander Le Saux,' Matthew said to her one day in the canteen, where he and Maisy had taken to sharing breakfast most mornings. This had started out as coincidence, with both of them arriving to eat just after six-thirty, and had proved so companionable that by unspoken agreement they now made it a permanant fixture in their working day. It gave them the opportunity to talk without fear of keeping patients waiting and for Matthew to answer any of Maisy's queries, which he seemed more than happy to do.

The only problem that *Maisy* had with this arrangement was a lack of concentration or, rather, she discovered that it was difficult to concentrate on the subject under discussion. She found those chiselled features of her boss far too big a distraction! A distraction she had been working very hard on subduing, but so far with little success.

'Leander and I have known each other since student days,' Matthew was saying, 'when I came over from Sydney to do my student elective here— and we've kept in touch ever since. He even made me best man at his wedding so the ticket over made it the most expensive wedding *I've* ever attended!'

'You can afford it,' joshed the paediatrician. 'You Aussie doctors are all rolling in money!'

'And I'd like you to meet Maisy Jackson,' continued Matthew. 'She's my new research registrar.'

Leander smiled. Like every paediatrician that Maisy had ever met, he had the kind of gentle, genuine smile which immediately put you at your ease. 'Hello, Maisy,' he said, shaking her hand vigorously. 'Your brother-in-law told me to keep an eye out for you. Thank goodness he didn't ask me to be responsible for your moral welfare, too, or I would have had to suggest that you didn't work with this dreadful Australian!'

Matthew laughed uninhibitedly. 'And just why are you eating breakfast here with this dreadful Australian instead of at home with the lovely Nicolette?'

For a moment a fleeting shadow briefly darkened the paediatrician's face. Maisy noticed, but she wasn't sure if Matthew had—he was busy spreading far too much marmalade onto a piece of toast.

'She went out very early this morning,' said Leander. 'For a walk, she said. She hasn't been sleeping too well recently.'

Something sombre in his voice made Matthew look up from his toast and frown, before saying hastily, 'So, tell me, Leander, are the rumours finally to be confirmed by the man himself? Is it official yet?'

'I'm afraid so. It's going out in the hospital newsletter at the end of the week.' The paediatrician pulled a comic face. 'I know that it's a great honour, and so on, but I'm still not entirely happy with the handle.'

'Leander has just been made Professor of

Paediatrics,' explained Matthew to a mystified Maisy.

'Oh, congratulations!' she beamed.

'Thanks very much,' he acknowledged with a smile. 'In fact, Nicolette is insisting that we have some sort of party to celebrate. Just an impromptu get-together this weekend. I hope you'll come, Matthew.' He looked from one to the other. 'In fact, why don't you both come? Bring Maisy with you. It'll give you a chance to meet a few people socially, Maisy.'

Maisy had felt Matthew stiffen beside her. 'I don't really think it's fair on Matthew—'

'Oh, nonsense!' contradicted Leander cheerfully. 'He could invite any woman in the hospital and they'd clamour to come with him. Only trouble is that they would be draped all over him, gazing into his eyes all ga-ga and completely monopolising him so that nobody else could get near him all evening. Leastways, that's what it used to be like in our wild student days, didn't it, Matt?'

'That was a long time ago,' answered Matthew ruefully. 'I don't know if I have the energy to be so wild now!'

Maisy decided that the only way to diffuse any resentment he might feel at *having* to take her would be by confronting it head-on. She patted the arm of his white coat and smiled up at him winningly.

'And how do you know that *I* won't be gazing into his eyes all evening?' she quizzed in a squeaky little-girl voice, while batting her eyelashes outrageously at him.

Both men laughed.

'Because you're much too sensible,' answered Leander. 'Your sister told me that.'

'*Did* she?' asked Maisy, surprised and somewhat intrigued because common sense where men were concerned was not something she had especially been known for up till now!

Leander nodded. 'She did. Said you'd just dumped your horrible fiancé. Is that right?'

Maisy blushed, partly because such a bald comment made her sound so *hard* and partly because she realised that her hand was still resting on Matthew's arm. She hastily withdrew it. 'Er, yes,' she stumbled. 'That's right.'

'Well, in that case you need a party to cheer you up,' said Leander firmly. 'See you on Saturday at about eight. Don't eat—we'll feed you.'

They watched him walk away, and eventually Maisy plucked up the courage to say, 'You don't *have* to take me, you know.'

Matthew gave her a deliberate look of bemusement. 'I do realise that,' he answered coolly, 'but it's just a casual get-together to toast a friend's good news. We might as well go along together— it's really no big deal, Jackson.'

Ouch! Hurt pride made it easy to copy his air of detachment. 'I wasn't suggesting for a moment that it was.' She shrugged, and glanced quickly at her watch. 'Hadn't we better go? We're due in clinic.'

'Of course,' he answered, aware that he had, in some subtle way, been rebuked by her. And the oddest thing of all was that he recognised that he had deserved it.

Over in clinic they saw Mrs Barnes, the earth mother whom they had originally suspected as having had peritonitis as a child. The hystero-dye had confirmed that first, tentative diagnosis, and she was due to begin IVF treatment.

'One of your Fallopian tubes is intact,' Matthew explained, 'and doesn't *appear* to have been affected by the infection. However, since nothing has happened so far we're going to go ahead with IVF.'

'Oh, thank you, Dr Gallagher!' beamed Mrs Barnes. 'Thank you so much!'

'It's very early days yet,' he warned, 'and you have a lot of time-consuming and disruptive treatment ahead of you. You're going to have to take drugs and have scans—and only when the conditions are perfect do we collect the eggs from you, fertilise them with your husband's sperm and then implant them back into your uterus.'

'I don't mind,' she said happily.

'And there is still no guarantee that it will work first time around,' he said.

'But it *is* going to work first time,' said Mrs Barnes fervently. 'I can feel it in my bones!'

Matthew smiled, unable to resist the woman's enthusiastic belief. 'Let's hope so.'

Next in were Mr and Mrs Sergeant, whom Maisy had witnessed having an embryo transfer on her first day. They were delighted with the confirmation that Angie was now pregnant with twins.

'We just can't believe our luck!' she told Matthew dreamily. 'Two babies!'

'It's a little more than luck,' observed Matthew wryly. 'You've had to work hard to get to this stage so just make sure that you take care of yourself from now on.'

Mrs Sergeant shot a glance at her husband, and smiled. 'Oh, I will, Doctor,' she sighed. 'Scott makes sure of that.'

'Breakfast in bed every morning,' he said. 'And no lifting.'

'So it was worth getting pregnant just for that!' joked his wife.

They had a steady stream of patients until lunchtime and then everything quietened down. Matthew was writing in a set of notes and Maisy sat opposite him reading up about clomiphene, a drug indicated for patients whose ovulation defect was associated with normal levels of oestrogen.

She was just making notes about which four groups of women benefited from this particular drug when Matthew looked up and said, 'So, have you thought any more about your research?'

Maisy blinked. 'My research?'

'Your research,' he echoed drily. 'That *is* what you're supposed to be here for, Jackson. Haven't you looked at those proposals I gave you yet?'

Her grey eyes were clear and candid. 'To be honest, Matthew, I've been too busy reading around the subject.'

Anybody else would have lied, bluffed or invented something, he thought half-exasperatedly.

'If I were a tyrannical kind of consultant I would haul you over the coals for admitting that.'

'But I've been learning so much from you,' she protested. 'How could I start researching something before I have all the background knowledge?'

He laughed in spite of himself. 'And did you also learn that such outrageous flattery would let you get whatever you wanted?'

Maisy shook her head and her blonde curls shimmered. 'It isn't outrageous, and it isn't flattery. It's true.'

'Nonetheless, I *am* flattered,' he told her gravely, 'but I would appreciate it if you gave some thought to what you wanted to look into. Perhaps you might get the opportunity to glance over those proposals by Saturday.'

'Saturday?' asked Maisy blankly.

She'd *forgotten*! he thought. She'd actually forgotten that they were supposed to be going out together. But Matthew mentally shrugged off this unexpected blow to his ego with more than a touch of amusement. 'We've been invited to Nicolette's and Leander's. Remember?'

She hadn't forgotten. She was simply taken aback that he planned to discuss *work* when they were supposed to be going to a *party*! But at least his words would prevent her from getting any ridiculous romantic notions where he was concerned. Matthew clearly saw their enforced 'date' as simply an extension of their working life. She wondered if perhaps she should wear her white coat—maybe even carry a stethoscope with her instead of a handbag! 'Of course I remember.'

'I'll pick you up at seven-thirty.'

'I'm in the doctors' mess,' she told him automatically. 'Room twelve.'

He didn't like to tell her that he already knew that. That he had been returning home late one evening about a fortnight ago and had seen her disappearing back into her room, her hair still wet from the shower and wearing a pale blue fluffy bathrobe which had made him have some fairly indecent thoughts about those luscious curves of hers. 'Make sure you're ready on time,' he warned. 'I hate being kept waiting.'

She doubted whether he had been kept waiting in his life. And especially not by a woman! 'I'll try, Matthew,' she told him sweetly.

And she *did* try. But fate, or so it seemed, conspired against her.

Since nothing in her wardrobe seemed remotely suitable Maisy had taken the bus into Southbury to buy a dress. But her mission had proved fruitless. Not only did she fall to find anything which didn't make her look like a kewpie doll—you had to be so careful when your hair was curly: anything involving velvet or lace couldn't even be considered—but she also got soaked in the most torrential downpour as she stood waiting for the bus back to the hospital.

Unfortunately the bus was very late, but this time there was no yellow sports car breezing conveniently by to offer her a lift.

It was almost seven by the time she arrived back in her room, and if she had done the sensible thing of simply towelling dry her hair and throwing on some fresh clothes then she might have been ready in time.

But one glance in the mirror made her decision easy. Where her dust-spattered hair had started to dry it looked like frizz, and the rain had streaked her mascara into black lines down her cheeks. She was *not* going to turn up at the Professor of Paediatric's party looking like a rag-bag!

And if Matthew Gallagher had to wait, then so be it! If he didn't like it she would follow on later.

She showered and washed her hair and examined her wardrobe once more, before finally deciding on an ankle-length dress in charcoal-grey linen. It wasn't in the least bit sexy, but it *was* beautifully cut.

She made her face up and was just blow-drying her hair when there was a knock at the door.

She switched off the hairdryer and opened the door, to see Matthew standing there. He was wearing brown cords and an oatmeal-coloured shirt, his brown hair newly washed and shiny—with a strand flopping onto his forehead that she found herself itching to smooth aside. He looked absolutely gorgeous, and Maisy felt quite overwhelmed by the sight of him.

'I have to finish drying my hair,' she said rather weakly. 'So, if you want to go on without me?'

She waited for a stern lecture about lateness, but there was none. Instead, he moved inside the room and nodded.

'Go ahead,' he said. 'I'll wait.'

For some extraordinary reason Maisy felt acutely embarrassed as she switched the hairdryer back on and began to vigorously brush her curls against the warm current of air. Giles had witnessed similar pre-party preparations many times, and she had not felt all fingers and thumbs as she did now. So what was the difference?

And why did it matter so much what he thought of her little home? Why did it fill her with a disproportionate amount of relief that she had brought sunflowers back from the market with her, and that they now blazed with colour and life on the windowsill in the blue and white pottery vase which she had splashed out on the week before?

Matthew felt curiously displaced, trying to focus his attention on the rather attractive little water colour which she had hung on one wall when, in fact, it was as much as he could do not to be mesmerised by the sweet swell of her bottom through the grey dress as she bent over the hairdryer.

He found that it was suddenly very difficult to think of Maisy as his registrar. He found that he wasn't thinking very much beyond how he would like to carefully remove that beautifully cut garment and to lie with her on that narrow bed and. . .

'Would you like something to drink?' she asked him.

He shook his head. If he added alcohol to the equation in this situation there was no knowing *what* might happen. 'No, thanks.'

There was an uncomfortable silence as she gave

the mop of curls a final brush. She picked up a shawl of softest black cashmere. 'Shall we go now?'

'Sure.' Automatically he helped her adjust the shawl around her shoulders, resisting the urge to run his finger along the long, vulnerable line of her pale neck.

It wasn't until they were outside that he felt something approaching normality, and was able to draw in a deep breath. 'Leander and Nicolette live on the cliff road,' he told her. 'We *could* drive but, to be honest, by the time we've parked it's just as quick to walk. And it's a beautiful evening.'

It was.

Side by side they walked through the golden evening, making conventional comments about the views and the sky and the sunset when all the time Maisy found herself wishing that he would do something unwise and wonderful—like pulling her into his arms and kissing her, as he had teasingly threatened to do when he had driven her home on her first day at Southbury.

But he did no such thing, and it was something of a relief to arrive at the large, white house with its paint palette of a garden.

'Isn't it beautiful?' asked Maisy softly, as she bent to crush a purple spear of lavender between her fingers. She tried not to feel wistful as she imagined living somewhere as lovely as this, with children running up and down the gravel paths which ran between the herb bushes.

Matthew watched as she lifted the crushed flower to her nose, closed her eyes and breathed in the scent deeply. She looked completely lost in thought. 'Your dream home?' he queried quietly.

Maisy grinned. 'I wouldn't mind.'

She wouldn't like Australia, then, he found himself inexplicably thinking. You couldn't get a more English garden than *this*. 'We'd better go inside,' he said gruffly.

Just as he lifted his hand to knock the front door was flung open and Maisy instantly recognised the tall paediatrician with the dark red hair.

What she did not expect was that she would also recognise the woman beside him, whose face he glanced down at so lovingly and who Maisy guessed was Nicolette, his wife.

Somehow she managed to keep her face composed and neutral as she faced the woman with the familiar face and the unforgettable ebony hair. The woman who she had seen sobbing so distractedly in the cathedral.

'Hi, Leander! Hello, Nicolette!' grinned Matthew, as he bent forward and placed a kiss on the woman's cheek. 'Nicolette, I'd like you to meet Maisy Jackson, who has just been admiring your beautiful garden.'

CHAPTER EIGHT

NICOLETTE turned her bright blue eyes towards Maisy. 'I could show you the garden properly, if you'd like,' she said tentatively.

'I'd like that very much,' smiled Maisy.

'And Matthew can help me with the drinks,' observed Leander.

Matthew's eyes crinkled at the corners. 'I'll help you drink them, sure!'

'Spoken like a true Aussie! Come on, Matt, I've got a houseful of guests waiting!'

The two women began to walk along a path which was lined with tiny pink daisies, with Maisy making occasional little cries of delight as she spotted different varieties of plants she would never have expected to see growing there in the garden's relatively exposed position.

'Those hedges were planted to act as a windbreak,' explained Nicolette, as she pointed to a leafy green wall behind them.

And it wasn't until they were some way away from the house that the subject which had been playing so heavily on both their minds was broached.

'Thank you for not saying anything about the other time we met,' said Nicolette in a low voice.

Maisy watched as the slim, dark woman hesitated

beneath a rose bower as the distant sounds of the party drifted out of the open French windows towards them. 'We didn't actually meet, though, did we?' she asked. 'We saw one another at the cathedral—'

'And I was sobbing.'

'Lots of women sob, Nicolette,' said Maisy gently.

Nicolette's mouth trembled. 'You still could have told someone.'

'It isn't my story to tell,' said Maisy firmly.

Nicolette rather nervously tipped her head to one side, her black hair spilling like corkscrews of satin over one shoulder and her blue eyes piercing and direct. 'Would you mind awfully if I asked your advice about something?' she asked slowly.

Maisy smiled. 'As a woman or as a doctor?'

'Both.' Nicolette's face was troubled now. 'But as a doctor most, I guess.'

'But you're married to a doctor,' Maisy pointed out.

'That's not the same.'

'No. I guess it's not.' Maisy agreed quietly, thinking of her own mother and father and remembering how her mother had told her that doctor husbands were often too emotionally involved to ever give their wives the best treatment.

'Ever since you saw me crying in the cathedral I've been half expecting to hear something from you,' whispered Nicolette, as though someone might be listening to them.

Maisy shook her head. 'It was none of my

business. Any dialogue should be instigated by you, not by me.'

Nicolette bit down on her lip with the expression of someone who had been bottling up a problem for a long time. 'That's very sweet of you. And somehow I knew that. But if I don't tell someone soon I think I'll go mad.' She stared down at the diamond ring which glittered on her wedding finger, and bit her lip. 'I think I may be sterile,' she whispered.

They were at a party—somebody could come out and disturb them at any moment. Of necessity, Maisy was succinct. 'Why?'

'We've been married two and a half years. We've never used any contraception—' Her voice began to wobble.

'You've had tests?'

'None.'

Maisy stared at the beautiful black-haired woman who stood framed by fragrant peach roses. 'So how on earth can you possibly come to a conclusion like that?'

Nicolette put the palm of her hand over her heart. 'Instinct,' she said brokenly.

Maisy shook her head firmly. 'Sorry, Nicolette, but I'm a medic and I've always been rather sceptical about instincts. What does Leander say about it?'

Nicolette briefly closed her eyes. 'We haven't discussed it.'

Maisy blinked with surprise. From what Matthew had been telling her on the way here, the paediatrician and his wife were besotted with each other. 'Why ever not?'

'Because I don't want to. I always shrug it off.'
She met the question in Maisy's eyes without flinching. 'Because if we acknowledge it to each other
then it will somehow make it real—'

'And if you don't talk about it then you won't be
able to find a remedy for it.'

'And what if there *is* no remedy?' asked Nicolette
in a low, fraught voice. 'What if we *can't* have a
baby when I know that Leander longs for one of
his own so much?'

'Then you learn to live with that fact,' Maisy told
her gently, as she remembered the words that she
had heard Matthew use to every single set of patients
who came to see him, 'and realise that life can be
full and loving without children. But burying your
head in the sand and having huge, unspoken fears
will drive a far greater wedge into your relationship
than learning to cope with childlessness ever would.
Have you spoken to Matthew about it?'

Nicolette shook her head. 'Oh, no! It seems too
personal to discuss with Matthew, even though it's
his speciality. He was our best man. I know him
too well. And how can I possibly tell Matthew something
which I dare not tell my own husband?'

'Would you let *me* talk to him?'

Nicolette blushed. 'I wouldn't feel happy about
Matthew examining me,' she protested.

Maisy laughed. 'Well, neither would I!' she confided. 'But he could always refer you both to another
clinic—'

'But Leander is always so busy—'

'He'll find the time for this,' said Maisy. 'You

know he will. Now, are you going to let me talk to Matthew about it?'

There was a long pause before Nicolette nodded. 'OK.'

'And, in the meantime, you *must* tell Leander about how you're feeling. Secrets can destroy a relationship. Promise me you'll talk to him.'

'I will,' Nicolette affirmed huskily. 'I promise.'

Their conversation was halted by Matthew walking towards them. He was carrying two glasses of champagne which he gave to them and his sage eyes crinkled at the corners as Maisy recoiled a little from the bubbles which shot up her nose.

'Not used to hard liquor, then, Jackson?' he murmured drily.

'Wanna bet?' she drawled smokily as she took a huge sip, and he laughed and so did she and neither of them seemed aware of Nicolette's narrow-eyed look in their direction.

The three of them walked back into the house where Matthew introduced Maisy to what seemed like scores of new people until her face ached with smiling.

This was not the time, she decided, to discuss Nicolette and her problems. She would ask him later on the way home.

So, instead, she put Nicolette's fears right out of her mind as she and Matthew joined a group of consultants and their wives and chatted and drank more champagne and then, after eating fish pie, Matthew went off in search of some pudding.

He really could be very easy company, Maisy

thought, suddenly becoming aware that several women were looking at her curiously—and very enviously—as he returned with two bowls full of strawberries.

Matthew was aware of the looks, too, and knew that just *taking* a woman to a party was normally enough to start wild speculation in the closed community of a hospital.

So why did he compound what the gossips were undoubtedly saying by taking Maisy very firmly by the hand and leading her to a big, high-ceilinged room, which had been cleared for dancing, and pulling her into his arms?

Because she was irresistible, that was why, he decided, as he felt her melt like a kitten against him. Because, in spite of those honeyed curls and innocent grey eyes, he suspected that Maisy Jackson had an innate sensuality that had never been tapped before.

And he wanted to be the one to tap it, he thought with a silent groan of frustration as she moved closer into the circle of his arms.

Maisy had never before been prey to the magic that a dance could weave around a couple—Giles had not liked dancing and had only ever danced with her under sufferance.

But now she found that her arms had wound sinuously around Matthew's neck, as though she had no conscious control over them. She was aware that she was behaving like some over-demonstrative limpet who refused to be prised away, and yet somehow she couldn't stop herself from breathing in the subtle, musky smell of him.

'You like dancing, don't you, Jackson?' he murmured appreciatively against her hair, and tightened his hands around her waist.

And Maisy was far too enraptured by the feel of his arms around her to do anything other than slumberously respond, 'It seems that I do.'

They stayed locked together like that for dance after dance. Until Matthew realised that he was beginning to want her very badly indeed, and that if he continued to dance so intimately with her then his desire would become impossible to hide. And instinct told him to back off where desire for Maisy Jackson was concerned.

'I think we've danced enough,' he said, a touch ruefully. Maisy knew exactly what he meant. She was no innocent, and she had been growing increasingly aware of Matthew's need for her—a need which she found herself reciprocating. But one which, ironically, she was now glad to relinquish.

She leaned back in his arms and smiled. 'I agree.'

He smiled back, ridiculously thrilled to meet a woman who could respond with restraint. He certainly hadn't met many of *those* in his life! 'More champagne?' he queried softly.

'Is that wise?'

'Who cares?' he retorted, and she laughed.

They drank some more and then Matthew introduced her to a cardiologist who was a great friend of her brother-in-law's, and they stayed chatting to him and his wife until almost midnight when

Matthew felt it was safe to make their escape. Then immediately he felt guilty for thinking it—after all, Leander was one of his best friends—but never had he felt less like being sociable than tonight. He wanted her alone, away from the necessity to make bright, social chatter.

Outside a warm breeze stirred the leaves into whispers, and the sound of breaking waves in the distance was soothing and hypnotic as they walked back down the cliff path towards the doctors' mess. Maisy felt as though she were floating on a great bubble of happiness, and tried to tell herself that it was the champagne and nothing more than that.

'Enjoy the party?' he asked.

'Very much. They seem like a lovely couple.'

'They are.' Matthew frowned. 'Though I must say that Nic doesn't quite seem herself lately.'

They had reached the door of her room and his remark seemed to spur Maisy into action. Why wait until tomorrow to tell him? It was only just past midnight. 'Would you like to come in for coffee?'

Infuriatingly, he felt the acid sensation of disappointment bittering his mouth. Was she just the same as every other woman he met? Did she want him to make love to her tonight?

'Do you think that's a good idea?' he asked repressively.

All the blood drained from Maisy's face. 'You don't drink coffee, then?' she queried, deliberately misunderstanding.

'That isn't what I meant—'

'No?' she questioned levelly. 'Then just exactly what *did* you mean?'

'Just that if I come into your room late at night with memories of what it was like having you in my arms on the dance-floor, well, it could be a little dangerous, don't you think?'

'What—and you just naturally assume that you're so sexy and I'm so responsive that we'll just tumble into bed together without a thought for the consequences?'

'That isn't what I meant—'

'That's *exactly* what you meant, Matthew Gallagher!' she stormed. 'And I can assure you that tumbling into bed with you was the *last* thing on my mind!' *Liar!* taunted the voice of her conscience, but she steadfastedly refused to heed it. She unlocked the door and pushed it open, then turned to him. 'You'd better come in for five minutes— what I have to say won't take long.'

Both bemused and intrigued by her persistence, Matthew followed her inside.

He indicated an easy chair. 'Shall I sit here,' he enquired gravely, 'or am I expected to start tumbling you onto the bed right away?'

Torn with a desire to laugh, coupled with a desire to either slap that arrogant face or kiss that divine mouth of his, Maisy glowered and he mockingly glowered right back.

She waited until he was seated and then she primly positioned herself in the chair opposite him, with her ankles crossed and her knees together, wondering if there was a discreet way to say what she had to and deciding that there wasn't.

'Nicolette asked me to speak to you,' she said without preamble. 'She and Leander haven't been using contraception for two and a half years and nothing has happened.'

He digested this in silence. 'Leander hasn't mentioned it to me himself,' he observed thoughtfully.

'That's because they haven't discussed it. With each other, I mean.'

Somehow she had correctly anticipated his righteous anger on hearing this.

'They *haven't*?' he demanded. 'Why the hell not? They're the closest couple I know.'

Maisy had thought hard about this. 'Because I think that superstition plays a huge part in having babies. Nicolette fears that if she discusses the problem with Leander then it will make it more real, whereas if she just keeps quiet then the problem might just go away and solve itself. It's an irrational fear, Matthew, but that doesn't make it any less real.'

'But why, in heaven's name, is she discussing it with *you*?' he demanded.

'Because I'm a woman?'

'Oh, really?' he mocked. 'If she were going to talk to anyone it should have been to me and not someone she's only just met. What price equality now, Jackson?'

'Oh, can't you understand anything, you *dense* man?' she exploded. 'You're a friend of theirs! And sometimes it's much easier to confide in someone you don't know because you feel that they aren't

judging you. You also happen to be a member of
the opposite sex—'

'So?'

'If you'll just listen I'll tell you!' She drew a deep
breath. 'Rightly or wrongly a lot of women, however
personally liberated they might be, feel very shy at
the thought of having all their private bits examined
by a friend of the family who happens to be a man!
How would you feel if Nicolette was a genito-
urinary surgeon who offered to take a look at your
testicles?'

Matthew couldn't help it—it was the last thing
he'd expected the prim Miss Maisy Jackson to come
out with. He burst out laughing. 'Point taken,' he
conceded once he had stopped laughing, and then
his face grew serious. 'So, why did she ask you in
particular?'

'I think she wanted some impartial advice from
a woman and a gynaecologist.'

'Which you gave?'

'I did.'

'And may I ask what you suggested?'

'I said that I would talk to you. And that you
could probably refer her to another treatment centre
for investigation.'

'She doesn't want to come here?' asked Matthew,
rather affronted now as professional pride got the
better of him. 'When it's the best bloody unit in the
south of England?'

'I'm sure she'd love to come here,' said Maisy
placatingly, 'if it weren't staffed by people who
know both her *and* her husband. All those tests. And

such intimate tests, too. Surely you can understand *that*, Matthew, and refer them to somewhere equally good? Somewhere where they won't be in the spotlight because they're medical and they're staff.'

'I'm not referring her *anywhere* until she talks it over with Leander,' said Matthew stubbornly.

He was both surprised and pleased when Maisy nodded and said, 'I agree.'

Their eyes met in a moment of total accord until Maisy remembered everything else that had happened and been said this evening. About beds and tumbling into them. And how easy it would be. . .

Colouring very slightly, she quickly stood up and smoothed down the skirt of her grey dress.

'Well, I won't keep you any longer, Matthew,' she babbled. 'Thank you for a lovely evening.'

He gave an enigmatic smile as he slowly rose to his feet. She looked quite exquisite standing there, he thought, with that mop of silken blonde hair contrasting with the severity of the grey dress which hinted at lush curves beneath. Far sexier than something revealingly tight, he decided, and a pulse in his cheek began to flicker.

He didn't stop to analyse his thoughts, just moved towards her until he was close enough to tilt her chin with the tip of one long finger and Maisy found herself imprisoned by that sage-green stare.

'Ah, Jackson,' he murmured, 'if only. . .'

'If only. . .what?' she queried breathlessly.

'If only your heart weren't still aching from your broken engagement—'

'It is *not* still aching!' she answered crossly. 'I'm over that.'

He stored this nugget of information away with a surprising amount of satisfaction. 'And if only we didn't work together. . .'

Her grey eyes widened. 'Then what?'

'Then I could kiss you to my heart's content.'

Afterwards she would be astonished that she had had the nerve to say with a slow challenge, 'Well, I'm not stopping you, Matthew Gallagher.'

'Ah, but grown-ups never stop at kissing,' he mused, forcing himself to be adult as he observed her pink cheeks and sparkling eyes. 'Do they? They fall into bed together and have relationships, and when those relationships break up they are forced to maintain a degree of civility in the workplace, which isn't always easy. Don't you agree, Jackson?'

Maisy shuddered with memory. Yes, she certainly did. She recalled working together in Theatres with Giles for those few weeks after they had split up when you could have cut the atmosphere with a knife.

And what had, seconds ago, seemed like the most delectable idea in the world—that of Matthew kissing her—now filled her with dread as she reminded herself that she was a total failure in bed.

Just imagine seeing the ensuing derision on Matthew's face, she thought in horror, if she was foolish enough to end up in bed with *him*.

Matthew had been about to leave when the expression on her face stalled him—an expression of such self-doubt that it chilled him to the bone.

Without thinking, he reached out and his arms went round her. His head bent down to hers as if it was the most natural thing in the world. Which, indeed, it was. This was kissing on a scale that Matthew was unused to.

There was no dazzling display of erotic technique, no threshing around of tongues. Instead, it was the sweetest kiss he had ever experienced—like a long draught of water after years spent in the desert. An intimacy which was all the more evocative for its restraint, and he frowned into her dazed face as he released her, sensing danger in her total lack of guile.

To Maisy his face merely looked forbidding in the aftermath, and she quickly moved away from him. It was pretty obvious to *her* that he regretted what had just happened, and so she struggled to say something which would salvage some of her wounded pride. 'Anyway,' she commented, 'maybe the truth of the matter is that *your* heart is still aching. . .'

As soon as the words were out of her mouth she regretted them for his face darkened and his mouth tightened into a grim line.

'And why should *my* heart be aching?' He shot each word towards her like a bullet.

She decided to brazen it out. 'Because you had a girlfriend back in Australia, didn't you?'

'I had several, actually,' came the sardonic reply. 'Was there one in particular to whom you were referring?'

Maisy racked her brain. 'Her name was Becca,' she said quietly. 'Wasn't it?'

'Yes. It was. So you've been listening to hospital gossip, have you?'

'Obviously.' She gave him a steady stare. 'Otherwise, how would I have known?'

His eyes blazed with verdant fire. 'I'm very disappointed in you, Jackson,' he bit out with derision.

'Well, don't be. I didn't go *searching* for information about you, if that's what you're implying. Someone went out of their way to tell me—but that doesn't mean to say that I believed every word of it.'

'And what did you hear?'

She listed the facts starkly. 'That you made a young and talented and beautiful doctor pregnant. And that you then abandoned her.'

'And?'

Maisy shrugged. 'That's it.'

He gave a bitter laugh. 'It's an interesting version of the facts—'

'You mean it's not true?'

He shook his head. 'It all depends on who is telling the story,' he observed acidly. 'Or who is interpreting it.'

Maisy looked at his troubled face, and her heart went out to him. 'Why don't *you* tell me the story, Matthew?' she suggested softly.

His expression was hunted, like that of a cornered animal. 'Why should I tell you anything?'

'Because I don't want to hear the interpretation that some arrogant young surgeon put on the facts,' she said. 'And maybe because I poured my heart out to you about Giles that first day so you owe me a confidence!'

He gave a smile which was bleak. 'In that case, I need a drink.'

'That bad, huh?' queried Maisy, as she hunted around for some whisky and glasses, and poured them both a measure.

'Bad enough.' He took the drink from her with the ghost of a smile and sipped at it thoughtfully, before sliding down into the chair once more and stretching his long legs out in front of him.

'So tell,' said Maisy softly, as she took her seat opposite him.

'These are the facts,' he said starkly, as if he were about to recite them in a court of law. 'I met Rebecca just under a year ago when she came to work at the hospital where I have been Consultant for the past three years.'

'And what's she like?' asked Maisy steadily, even though a murderous, black jealousy was threatening to rear its ugly head.

'Physically, you mean?'

'If you like,' she replied, with an effort.

'She's tall and very striking to look at—she could have easily chosen a career in modelling if she didn't have the intellectual capacity of a nuclear physicist.'

Maisy felt like a balloon which had just been deflated by a sharp pin. 'She sounds perfect,' she said woodenly.

'No one is perfect, Jackson,' he answered quietly, 'but Rebecca had a lot going for her.' He hesitated.

'And?'

'And, as I mentioned earlier, I have always made it a rule not to date people I work with—I've seen too many casualties to risk it,' he added wryly.

'But—let me guess—you decided to make an exception in her case?'

'You could put it that way,' he agreed reluctantly. 'Rebecca had been used to men falling at her feet— it's one of the consequences of outstanding beauty and talent—and so she couldn't handle it when I didn't do the same.'

Maisy screwed her nose up with hopeful confusion. 'You mean that you didn't fancy her?'

He gave the question some thought. 'It's a little more complex than that. I found her very attractive and I admired her brain, but. . .'

'What?'

'I had no burning desire to possess her, nor really to extend the boundaries of our relationship beyond our mutually agreeable association at work.'

'Well, *something* must have happened to change your mind, Matthew.'

'I guess.' He threw her a rueful glance. 'Call it arrogance—or pride—but every man in the hospital wanted Rebecca—'

'And she wanted *you*,' interrupted Maisy slowly. 'How did you know that?'

She gave him a look of exasperation. 'You would hardly need to be clairvoyant to work that out! Human beings respond to a challenge—and if she was the sort of woman who could have anyone then it stands to reason that she would want the one person who didn't want her. So you succumbed to her charms. . .'

'If you like. I saw it simply as breaking one of my rules. And at first the relationship was perfectly satisfactory, but—'

It struck Maisy that she would have been *mortified* to have her relationship with someone described as *satisfactory*!

'But what?' she prompted.

He looked at her steadily. 'It was a one-sided relationship.'

Well, she wasn't letting him get away with *that*! Maisy knew from her brother, Benedict, how most men would try to get by without admitting to emotions unless you gave them a gentle shove in the right direction. 'And what exactly do you mean by that?'

He sighed. 'What she felt for me was not reciprocated.'

'You mean you didn't love her in the way that she loved you?'

'Exactly.'

She looked at him expectantly. 'And?'

'I don't think she believed me when I told her that I didn't have the same depth of feeling. When you are a woman like Rebecca—used to getting everything you've ever wanted in life—rejection is something you simply can't countenance.'

'She wanted you—'

'She wanted me and she used the oldest trick in the book to make sure she would get me—'

'You mean she *deliberately* became pregnant?' asked Maisy, aghast.

The look he gave her now was gentle. 'When someone is a doctor, with a splinteringly high IQ and a career which is firmly on the ascendant, you don't get pregnant by mistake.'

'Were you angry?'

He paused. 'I experienced a mixture of emotions, the predominant one being sadness that this whole situation had got so badly out of hand, but I would be a liar if I denied that anger wasn't one of them. Yes, I was angry.'

Maisy drew a deep breath. It was painful to listen to, yes, but the fact that he was so readily confiding in her gave her a kind of strength. 'What happened?'

'At first I felt that I owed it to my unborn child to try and make a go of it with Rebecca so we moved in together, and it was then that I realised. . .' His face became contorted with a profound look of regret. 'I realised that I just didn't love her,' he said heavily. 'And that I never would—and certainly not in a way that would sustain our relationship in the many years which would lie ahead.'

'You told her that?'

'I tried to explain it in a way which would cause the least pain—'

'An impossible task?' queried Maisy quietly.

He flinched. 'As you say, an impossible task. I made it clear that I would support her and the baby in any way that I could, but that I could not stay with her as a couple. Rebecca took it badly—very badly indeed. It was still very early on in the pregnancy—'

'Weren't you worried that she wouldn't want to keep the baby, having heard that?' Maisy asked tentatively.

He hesitated. 'To be honest, the thought that she might do that made my blood run cold because, although I was a reluctant father, I *was* still a father and part of me wanted the baby so much.' He looked directly into Maisy's eyes.

'But I had no right to influence her judgement in any way, which is why I told her the truth about us as soon as I was certain. Because the decision on whether or not to keep the baby had, ultimately, to be Rebecca's. And, thank God, she chose to continue with the pregnancy, although her resentful feelings towards me only intensified.'

'What happened?'

'She began to attempt to blacken my name—'

'And was that damaging to you?'

He shook his head. 'I wasn't judged and found wanting by those who knew me. I had worked there as a student and during my early internship. My professional and personal reputation did not suffer unduly, but the atmosphere that Rebecca's allegations created made it very difficult for everyone concerned. I thought it best to absent myself for a while—'

'And that's why you agreed to the six-month swop with Jamie?'

He nodded. 'That's right.'

'And the baby?' she asked tentatively.

'Will be born around the time I am due back.'

'And will you not be there for the birth?'

'Rebecca doesn't want me there. Unless I am willing to make a commitment to her—a commitment which I have steadfastedly told her is not an option.'

'I see.' Hence his reluctance to get involved with her, and, really, thought Maisy, who could blame him? A great wave of sadness washed over her.

'And so, you see, when I came to England the very last thing on my mind was emotional attachment. I find you a very attractive woman, Jackson— intellectually *and* physically—but I don't want to take it any further. Can you understand that?'

Maisy did. And on a much deeper, instinctive level she also understood that she could feel very deeply for this man—in a way which would make her feelings for Giles seem like just scraping the surface of true affection.

But she also knew that Matthew was vulnerable now, and hurting. He had been rushed and hurried by a woman he didn't love, and he would be wary. If Matthew Gallagher decided that he wanted *her*, Maisy, then it must be without haste and totally of his own volition. To have a chance with him she must first have the strength to let him go.

But not completely. . .

She finished her whisky and put the glass down.

'Have I shocked you?' he enquired, as he did the same.

'Do I look so easily shocked, then?'

'No, you don't. Which surprises me in view of

that permanent air of innocence you seem to wear.'

She smiled. 'My brother discovered that he had a daughter years after she had been born. After finding *that* out nothing ever seemed to shock me again.'

And Benedict had married the mother of his child. That, too, was a possibility in this situation which Maisy must face. They said that blood was thicker than water. Matthew was so certain in his mind now what he wanted to do but when he saw his baby might he not decide that he could bear a life with the beautiful, talented Rebecca in order to keep that baby? She forced the thought away. 'Actually, the older I get less and less about life amazes me—'

'And you must be all of twenty-five, I guess?' he mocked softly.

'Twenty-seven, actually.' She drew a deep breath and took all her courage into both hands. 'Listen, Matthew, I've just ended a relationship, too, and the last thing I really need is to begin another one. But I'd like us to be friends—nothing more than that. If you think that's possible.'

'I think it would be uniquely possible,' he murmured with a slight pang, thinking how she was unlike any any other woman he had ever met. So easy. And so honest.

'Good.' Maisy's tone was brisk through necessity. 'I'll get Nicolette to phone you tomorrow, shall I?'

'Do.'

It was the hardest thing she had ever had to say. 'And now I'm going to kick you out.'

He was warm and he was comfortable. More than that, for the first time in longer than he could remember he actually felt some peace of mind. Leaving now was the last thing he wanted to do, but she was right—damn her! She was right.

He levered himself to his feet. 'Goodnight, Jackson,' he said.

'Goodnight, Matthew,' she gulped, and watched as he let himself out into the chill midnight air.

CHAPTER NINE

WHEN Maisy went to work early on the Monday morning following Matthew's astonishing revelation she felt as nervous as a child on her first day at school, but she put on a brave face and hoped that she was doing her best to hide it.

She had spent most of Sunday exploring Southbury and trying not to think about Matthew or Rebecca or their unborn baby—but it hadn't been easy.

She was dreading his reaction to seeing her, but when she appeared in the darkened room to begin the early-morning scanning and saw his tall, shadowed figure there he merely looked up and smiled, and said, 'Hello, Jackson,' in a quiet voice into which it was impossible to read anything other than what sounded like genuine pleasure to see her.

'We'd better get started,' he added, as he flicked through the long list of patients in his hand. 'We've got a busy day ahead of us.'

'Ready when you are,' she responded softly, all the tension immediately leaving her body. It seemed that he had meant it, then—their ability to be friends. It had not just been a careless promise made at the end of an emotional evening.

Maisy had also been to see Nicolette after the party, dropping off a small posy of flowers pur-

chased from the hospital shop. Ostensibly these were
to thank her for her hospitality but in reality she
wanted to tell her what Matthew had said about the
couple's failure to conceive, aware that she would
be unable to say anything at all if Leander was
around.

But Nicolette had been alone, a dark smudge of
dust shadowing the side of her nose, and had insisted
on Maisy joining her for coffee.

Maisy shook her head. 'No, I won't stop that
long, thanks. You're busy.'

'I'm not! Not now, anyway. Oh, *please*!'
Nicolette had beseeched with a sunny grin. 'We've
just finished the last of the clearing up, and
Leander's gone out for a ten-mile run—he's training
for the marathon, worse luck! Meanwhile, I'm
desperate for an excuse to sit down so you must
stay. I insist!'

So Maisy had been persuaded to drink fragrant
coffee and eat cherry cake in the Le Sauxs' bright
blue and white kitchen. 'I spoke to Matthew last
night,' she said, through a mouthful of moist cake
crumbs, 'and he says he's happy to refer you anywhere you like but that you must talk to
Leander first.'

Nicolette had blushed prettily right up to the roots
of her ebony curls. 'I told him last night,' she
answered softly. 'We had a long talk after everyone
had gone.'

'And was he cross? That you hadn't said anything
before?'

Nicolette gave the contented smile of a woman

who is truly loved. 'He isn't very good at being cross—especially with me. He blamed himself for not having broached the subject earlier when he suspected that I was troubled by the fact that I hadn't conceived. But he *had* tried to talk about it. . .' She sighed. 'And every time he tried I brushed the subject aside and started droning on about letting nature take its course and the fact that I was still very young.'

'Which you are,' smiled Maisy.

'Yes, I know. But I can't keep burying my head in the sand and thinking that we can wait for ever to find out simply because I *am* young. Leander also told me that if we can't have children then we'll adapt—or adopt! And that whatever happens I'm never going to bottle my feelings up again simply because I don't want to worry him. He says it's *far* more worrying if I do that!'

And Maisy had finished her coffee, feeling pleased for them both and more than a little bit envious.

'Speaking of Matthew,' Nicolette added, as she saw Maisy to the door, 'you and he seemed to be getting on very well on the dance-floor last night!'

'Er. . .yes.'

'He monopolised you all evening!'

'Did he?' asked Maisy, wondering why her breathing had gone so oddly shallow.

'You know he did! Now, if *I* were single and not madly in love with Dr Le Saux,' Nicolette had confided impishly, shooting Maisy a curious look, 'then Matthew Gallagher is the man I would want to get to know a bit better.'

'You and the entire female staff of Southbury Hospital, you mean?' Maisy had managed to joke weakly, before setting off on the cliff path back down to the doctors' mess.

She had suspected that being friends with Matthew would be easier said than done, and that perhaps he would regret having confided in her about Rebecca.

But her fears soon proved unfounded.

He seemed to go out of his way to be pleasant and courteous towards her and, as a teacher, his knowledge was daily proving invaluable.

On the Friday at the end of her first fortnight they had just finished doing the egg collection for Monday morning's embryo transfers when he asked her to come to his office.

He was sitting behind his desk, signing papers, when she knocked and he looked up and said, 'Sit down, Jackson, I'll be with you in a moment.'

She sat in silence, wondering what he was about to say. She watched the shiny, dark head bent over his papers, and bit her lip.

She had been doing her best to wean herself off having silly romantic notions about him and with a great deal of success, too. But sitting here, able to watch him unobserved, she acknowledged the almost painful lurching of her heart as it thundered out the rhythm of sexual attraction.

It was probably all for the best, she decided. She

had recognised from her very first day at Southbury that she was overwhelmingly attracted to her boss. And she certainly wasn't being naïve since she recognised that he felt something similiar for her, too. As a doctor, she knew enough about body language to be able to tell that he certainly wasn't immune to her as a woman.

If he hadn't had the complications back home then who knew what might have happened?

Except that there was a side to Maisy which was glad that the non-existent situation hadn't been put to the test. For what if history had repeated itself? What if she had failed him in bed as she had failed Giles? Wouldn't working with him then have become intolerable?

He looked up and put his pen down. 'So, Jackson,' he said at last, 'now that you're familiar with the working operation of the clinic have you given much thought as to which of the three research proposals you would most like to work on?'

She had been expecting the question, and had subsequently spent most of her evenings giving thought to this very subject. 'Actually, yes,' she told him. 'I have.'

He gave a brief nod of satisfaction. 'And?'

'I'd like to look into the effects of ageing on successful ovulation,' she said firmly.

He leaned back in his chair, the sage-green eyes narrowed so that Maisy was unable to read their expression. 'Remind me,' he murmured.

Maisy was certain that he was just testing her to see whether she had studied the proposal in depth.

'I want to find out whether the eggs of a thirty-eight-year-old woman are less good—less viable, I should say—than the eggs of, say, a twenty-eight-year-old woman.'

'And how would you go about doing that?'

'I would need to compare the proportion of women in their late thirties who have successful IVF treatment with women in their mid-twenties who have successful IVF treatment.'

'And when you say successful—'

'I mean treatment resulting in a pregnancy.'

'And it's topical, Jackson,' he murmured. 'Very topical. With women increasingly delaying child-bearing—'

'Due to careers or financial necessity—yes, yes, yes,' said Maisy impatiently, forgetting for a moment who she was speaking to. 'But wouldn't it be *wonderful* if we could prove that age was of no consequence and that women in their thirties and forties were just as damn good as their more youthful counterparts?'

'Careful, Jackson,' he admonished drily. 'I'm afraid that I could not possibly support your research proposal if I suspected that you were going to allow feminist principles to distort your investigations.'

'Don't be silly, Matthew,' she responded primly. 'If doctors allowed principles to affect their treatment they would refuse to treat corrupt politicians!'

He gave a brief laugh. 'And how do you intend to begin?' he asked suddenly, switching the subject completely.

'I'll need to think about the methodology quite

carefully. Obviously, the conditions must be the same for both groups,' she began, waving her hands around in the air—carried away with enthusiasm. 'You see. . .'

Matthew smiled as he sat back in his chair, and listened.

It took Maisy only two weeks to get approval from the ethics committee to begin her research. She had to submit details about the finance she would need, the equipment she would require and the number of patients who would make up her sample.

On the day she learnt that she had her approval and that research could begin Maisy brought a bottle of champagne into the clinic and shared it with some of the staff, including Staff Nurse Marsh whose attitude to Maisy had softened—presumably once she had discovered that Maisy was soon to have her own separate little office right down at the opposite end of the corridor from Matthew's!

'Who's your research supervisor?' queried one of the embryologists.

'I am,' said Matthew, and lifted his plastic cup of champagne to her in a toast.

Maisy raised her cup back and managed to smile, acutely aware that such a meaningless gesture from him should not have made her pushed her pulse rate up into the danger zone!

And once she had imposed some kind of structure into her new working day Maisy began living the kind of life that she had always intended to live. A life where hard work dominated in a satisfying way—in a way it had never done before.

As a medical student she had been too busy going out enjoying herself to commit herself to anything in the way of research, and as a house officer she had had her work cut out just to keep up with all the demands of a busy new career. Then she had become engaged and her life had seemed to be dominated by shopping for the ingredients for a fussy fiancé's supper!

But now she was up every morning before the alarm went off, ready to join Matthew in the canteen for breakfast.

Here he would ask her in detail about her progress, and also alert her to any cases or clinics of his she might like to look in on. These were not necessarily of any use to her research, but of sufficient rarity or interest to increase her broader knowledge of infertility treatments.

He also kept her up to date with the patients she already knew. Through Matthew she learnt that Mrs Williams—the ambitious career woman who had neglected to follow her treatment properly—had decided that she was going to cut back on her workload. Instead of climbing to the top of the corporate ladder, she now intended to put most of her energies into completing her IVF treatment successfully.

Maisy was surprised but pleased.

'So, what made her change her mind?' she asked Matthew softly.

He shrugged. 'She felt that the pressure on her was now off and, consequently, had a complete change of heart about her attitude to the treatment.'

'Just like that?'

'Just like that!' He smiled and gave an exagger-
ated sigh of puzzlement. 'Such contrary creatures,
you women!'

She might have made an indignant denial of this,
had she not remembered his pregnant girlfriend who,
it sounded, had been *extremely* contrary. A sensitive
subject, Maisy decided, and one which might cause
him added pain. She nodded as she sipped her tea,
but said nothing.

'And do you remember Mr and Mrs Paul?'
Matthew asked, giving her a hard, narrow-eyed look
as he cut into a generous portion of eggs and bacon.

Maisy smiled. Some patients you would never
forget! 'Ross and Kerry? He had an amazing South
London accent and mended radios?'

'That's right,' said Matthew, as he dabbed a
finger of toast into his egg.

'Yes, of course I remember them. Chronically
short of money but a really nice couple.'

'Very nice couple,' he agreed. 'And their treatment has been successful—on the second attempt.
Mrs Paul is now pregnant and they haven't bled the
bank account completely dry!'

'Oh, but that's wonderful!' enthused Maisy, wishing, not for the first time, that clinics could afford
to provide the expensive treatments free.

The mouthwatering smell of crispy bacon invaded
her nostrils and she sniffed appreciatively.

'Would you like some of this, Jackson?' he
quizzed, as he jabbed a rasher with his fork and

waved it in her direction. 'Or are you just going to sit there drooling?'

'I'd absolutely love some, but I'd better not,' she answered reluctantly. Her brother's birthday was coming up and he and his wife were throwing a party. And Maisy's party dress was already *very* clinging! 'Honestly, Matthew, I don't know how you can get away with eating a huge breakfast every morning—'

'And still keep my fabulous physique?' he teased.

It might not have been the most *modest* thing he could have said but it happened to be true. 'Something like that,' she agreed wryly.

'I exercise daily,' he murmured. 'That's how.'

For some absurd reason Maisy felt her cheeks grow hot. No, it wasn't absurd, she realised. She had been thinking of quite a different kind of exercise than the one to which he was obviously referring! 'D-do you jog?' she questioned hurriedly.

Did he recognise the source of her discomfiture? Was that why he smiled at her so roguishly? 'Sometimes,' he answered. 'Or I swim. Sometimes I play squash—or tennis. Cross-training—that's what we call it. You should join me some time.'

'You're saying that I need to lose some weight?'

'Such a predictable feminine response!' He threw her a sardonic glance. 'No, I'm saying that you should do some exercise—it's good for your heart and lungs! Your figure is fine,' he added, his eyes casually flicking over her.

'Th-thanks,' she stumbled stupidly, and then immediately felt cross with herself. As if no one had ever paid her a compliment before!

'So how about tonight? I'm swimming at Southbury Leisure Centre at seven-thirty. We could grab a bite to eat afterwards.' He must have seen her look of bemusement, for he added softly, 'We did agree to be friends, didn't we, Jackson?'

'Yes,' she gulped, 'we did.'

'And isn't that the kind of thing that friends do?'

'Yes, I suppose it is,' she answered shyly.

The evening went spectacularly well, even if Maisy did grow hot and uncomfortable at the sight of Matthew's half-naked body diving into the pool and ploughing through the turquoise waters with all the strength and grace of an Olympic swimmer.

Afterwards they found a tiny, old-fashioned bistro and ate steak and salad and a death-by-chocolate pudding, and he made her laugh more than she could remember having laughed for a long time.

All in all it had been a perfect evening, except that there was no goodnight kiss at the end of it. But, then, if there had been he probably would have expected more than that. And then he would have found her out. . .

Somehow, by a mutual but unspoken agreement, their outings became more frequent as summer slipped inexorably into a crisp and golden autumn.

Conkers lay brown and glossy on the dew-soaked grass as they went to the theatre and cinema together. Twice they travelled out into the nearby countryside to Arundale House, where classical concerts took place in the magnificent ballroom there.

All these cultural activities made sport take rather a back seat, and Maisy soon realised that the easy and relaxed relationship which was evolving between them was rare indeed. But short-lived, too, she thought with a sudden pang of regret.

As the days passed it became impossible to forget that soon Matthew would be returning to Sydney. To Rebecca. And to their baby.

Soon he would no longer be here, she reminded herself, no longer working just a few doors away. There would be no Matthew at breakfast, and no Matthew to help her solve problems—to help her put her muddled scientific thoughts into some semblance of order.

Increasingly, she found herself stealing a secret glance at him when he was unaware of her attention. She would gaze longingly at that strong, chiselled profile and the lazy curve of his smile, as if trying to print it indelibly on her mind so that she could take it out on long, lonely winter evenings and cherish it.

All the leaves fell and the bare branches of the trees were transformed into intricate fretwork, set against the pale blue of the winter sky.

December arrived at last and, though heavily discouraged by the ward sisters, junior nurses succeeded in decking the walls with paper streamers and sprigs of holly far earlier than they should have done. In the assisted conception clinic Staff Nurse Marsh spent an inordinate amount of time carefully dressing a small (and, in Maisy's opinion, rather ugly) silver Christmas tree.

One Saturday, about a week before the dreaded day when Matthew was due to fly home, he called her in to help him deal with an emergency admission.

Maisy was supposed to be off duty and had been trying to decide what to wear to her brother's party that night, but when the call came she rushed straight down to meet Matthew in Accident and Emergency.

He looked up from the notes briefly, then began talking as he continued to write. I have a Mrs McNamara in cubicle three,' he told her. 'She had her first IVF treatment earlier this month. She has now presented with diarrhoea, nausea and increasing breathlessness. She is also severely bloated and a first physical examination showed ascites. Any ideas what it might be, Jackson?'

'She could have ovarian hyperstimulation syndrome,' she answered immediately. 'Too much oestradiol in her system, causing an electrolyte imbalance?'

He nodded. 'Good. That's what I think too. And is it dangerous?'

'It carries a two per cent death rate. So, yes.'

'Treatment?'

'Initially, a full blood count and urea and electrolytes, which will doubtless show the electrolyte imbalance,' she said quickly. 'We need to drain the ascites and put up an albumen transfusion to correct any protein loss. After that we treat the symptoms systemically.'

'Going to stay and help me?' he asked, sage eyes glinting.

'Oh, yes, please,' she answered happily, not caring that the A and E staff nurse gave a knowing smirk at her junior.

It was gone six by the time the woman was out of danger, and as they washed their hands together at the sink Matthew saw Maisy sneak a worried glance at her watch.

'Going out?' he queried.

'Er. . .yes.' She had been *dying* to invite him but you couldn't really ask a man to meet your family, not when you weren't even going out with him!

'But you're running late?'

'That's right.'

'Need a lift somewhere?' he enquired casually. 'Or is someone picking you up?'

'No. I'm going on my own,' she told him primly, determined that there should be no misunderstanding. 'I was going to take the train.'

'Then why don't I drive you?'

'Because it's miles away.'

'I don't mind.' He saw her frown, and nodded understandingly. 'But I might cramp your style? Right?'

'Oh, *no*!' she cried in alarm. 'But it's my brother's birthday party, and I thought that. . .that. . .'

'That what?' he asked gently.

'That you'd be bored.'

He laughed. 'I haven't been bored with you *once*, Jackson. Not once. And that really is a first for me.'

'Matthew Gallagher, you are an arrogant, *arro-*

gant man!' she accused, but she was laughing too.

'No, just a fundamentally honest one!' he protested, putting his palm flat against his heart in an over-the-top gesture of sincerity. 'So, am I invited?'

'You know you are!' she sighed with pleasure, much against her better judgement.

Maisy's parents' home was only fifty miles away, but even though Matthew drove the yellow sports car at top speed as much as possible they were delayed first by rain and then roadworks, and it was almost ten o'clock by the time they drew up in front of the elegant, double-fronted house.

Maisy bit her lip and Matthew gave her a sideways glance.

'Does it matter, then, if we're late?'

'It's a sit-down meal. They won't mind. It's just. . .'

'Just what, sweetheart?'

Maisy heart skipped a beat at his use of the endearment, but some deeply buried instinct told her not to react to it. 'They didn't like Giles and they thought that he hurt me so they're a bit anti Maisy's men at the moment. Not that I've ever brought many back,' she elaborated, with an honesty that touched Matthew's heart. 'And I'll explain that we're not an item, or anything like that, but just in case my brother starts giving you the third degree—'

'I'll convince him that I have your best interests at heart,' he reassured her, pushing his hands deep into the pockets of his trousers and wishing that he could pull her into his arms and kiss those sweetly innocent-looking lips. But it would be a monstrously unfair thing to do, given the mess his life was in right now. Especially to a woman like Maisy. 'Don't worry, Jackson! I'm big enough to look after myself.'

As she rang the doorbell Maisy felt a little bit like a fly poised on the edge of a Venus fly-trap, and they walked in to the dining-room to find eighteen sitting down to dinner, with two places spare.

At opposite ends of the table!

Eighteen pairs of eyes looked up from their chicken forestière and were fixed on them with interest.

'Good luck,' muttered Maisy to Matthew as she went to kiss her mother and give her brother his birthday present. 'You'll need it!'

But the evening was a remarkable success. There were peals of laughter from Matthew's end of the table, where he seemed to be regaling the assembled company with a series of dry, witty jokes.

And her father liked him. So did Benedict—and Verity, his wife. Her mother whispered that she thought he was the most gorgeous man she had ever seen, but this came as no surprise to Maisy as the two of them had always had very similar tastes.

'Just don't let Dad hear you say that!' she whispered back with a giggle.

They travelled home late, with Matthew's favourite jazz spilling sweet, sultry notes into the car, and it wasn't until he had walked Maisy to her door in the doctors' mess that he turned to her and said, 'Did you realise that next week is my last week?'

Did she *realise*? Maisy stared at him incredulously. Hadn't it been looming over her like a great black cloud for weeks now? Was the man dense or merely very unobservant?

Maisy opened her mouth to ask him, but as she looked at his furrowed brow in the moonlight her mouth softened with sympathy as she thought of what lay ahead for him.

Because he had to go back to Australia. To a woman he said he did not love but a woman, nonetheless, who was the mother of his unborn baby. And, as such, that woman had a unique power over the man Maisy realised she had grown to love herself over the past weeks.

'Of course I realised,' was all she said in reply to his question.

Matthew saw the softening of her wide mouth, could read the compassion and understanding in her eyes and it was as much as he could do not to bury his head in her breast and seek solace there.

But he could not. Would not.

'I have to sort out my affairs,' he said abruptly. He hesitated for no more than a second before giving her one of his swift, sweet kisses.

'Of course you do,' said Maisy, dazed by the brush of his lips against hers.

And then he was gone, and Maisy was left staring after him, her fingers still touching her mouth where he had kissed it as she uttered a silent prayer that he would come back to her one day.

CHAPTER TEN

'OH, FOR goodness' sake, Maisy, why don't you come? Jamie and I both want you to—and you know most of the other guests! We've only been back a fortnight and everything is such a mess that I need you to help me serve drinks and things. Oh, come on—you can't mope around like a trainee nun on New Year's Eve!'

'I wasn't intending to mope around,' Maisy answered with a patient smile as she watched her pregnant sister move awkwardly around the small sitting room. It really was ironic, she decided, that when she had first arrived at the hospital she had longed for the company of her sister, Sarah, and Jamie, her husband. And now. . .

Now?

Now she was simply longing for the company of the tall, enigmatic Australian, who had crept so slowly and so completely into her heart that she felt like a hollow shell without him.

'Well, you can't just sit in on your own all night,' said Sarah briskly, wincing a little as she caught sight of her bulky frame in the mirror. 'I can't *believe* I've got another three weeks to go!'

'You *are* very big,' conceded Maisy, with a smile.

'Don't change the subject! I'd like to know what you're planning to do tonight,' Sarah demanded.

'There's my research—'

'Oh, there's *always* your research!' scoffed Sarah. 'Are you expecting to win the Nobel Prize with this particular piece of research, Maisy?'

Maisy bit her lip to stop it from trembling and glowered at her little sister. 'Why are you being so horrible to me?'

'Because I can't bear to see history repeating itself, that's why! You broke your heart over that worthless creep, Giles, and now you're doing exactly the same over Matthew Gallagher! Honestly, Maisy, sometimes I *do* wonder about you!'

'I did not,' said Maisy, with icy dignity, 'break my heart over Giles. Giles was a mistake from beginning to end, and one which I am very glad to be rid of.'

'Well, that's good,' remarked Sarah, only slightly mollified. 'And what about Matthew?'

Maisy drew a deep breath. 'Matthew's different. Matthew is very special, but I'm afraid I'm just going to have to wait and see what happens.'

'But why? *Why*?'

'I don't want to talk about it now.'

'Oh, Maisy, darling,' Sarah pleaded, 'please don't get hurt.'

It may be too late for that, thought Maisy ruefully. 'I shall try my very best *not* to get hurt, Sarah,' she replied with dignity.

Sarah hesitated. 'You know he made his girlfriend pregnant?' she asked uncomfortably.

Colour rushed hotly into Maisy's cheeks. 'Yes. I know that. But, in fact, your information is a little out of date. His girlfriend—or, rather, his *ex-*girlfriend—had the baby a week ago. A little boy named Samuel. He rang to tell me.'

It had been the briefest and most unemotional of phone calls, and whilst she had felt honoured that he had rung to tell her himself his clipped, far-away tones had left her feeling distinctly uneasy.

Sarah frowned with perplexity. 'You *knew* all that? Then why in heaven's name did you get involved with him—?'

'*Why*?' Maisy turned on her sister. 'Do I have to write it in letters of stone for you, Sarah Brennan? Because I love him, that's why! And I'm miserable without him and that's why I don't want to come to your wretched party tonight and pretend to be happy when I'm *not*!'

Sarah knew when to quit. Maisy's temper was rare but it was legendary, and she certainly wasn't staying around to see it in full flood! 'OK, OK! Point taken. I'm going! But if you feel like wandering down later to see the New Year in then do.'

Maisy suppressed a shudder. She was dog-tired, and had planned to have a large measure of whisky at around ten o'clock. Hopefully, that should knock her out well before midnight! 'I might,' she said, and gave Sarah a quick hug. 'And please don't worry about me!'

'But I *do*!'

After Sarah had gone Maisy took a long shower and afterwards dressed in some fleecy yellow pyjamas, bought more for warmth and comfort than for glamour. She ate smoked salmon sandwiches and drank coffee, and afterwards poured herself a large glass of whisky.

She was just sitting and sipping it when there was a knock at the door, and she clicked her tongue with irritation. If that was Sarah again, trying to drag her over to their party. . .

She flung the door open, all speech and reason deserting her when she saw just who stood in the darkness before her.

'Hello, Maisy,' came the familiar deep, lazy drawl. 'Aren't you going to invite me in?'

'Yes, yes. . .of course,' she managed, in a sudden burst of breath as she realised that he had called her Maisy. *Maisy*! Not Jackson. . .

'You've been drinking,' he said mildly as passed close by her and shut the door behind him. He took off his overcoat and draped it over the back of a chair. 'Drowning your sorrows?'

'Inducement to sleep, actually. You haven't quite driven me to the bottle *yet*, Matthew Gallagher!' she corrected him acidly, and he laughed. The laugh broke some of the tension. 'Would you like a drink?' she asked, and waved her hand vaguely in the direction of the whisky bottle.

He shook his head. 'I'd love some coffee, but not yet. Let's sit down first.'

He gestured to the sofa beneath one of the windows and Maisy sat down beside him, but not touching him. She did not dare to touch him. She had left the curtains undrawn and only one small lamp on, and silver moonlight spilled into the room with a ghostly radiance. Maisy shivered.

The speech he had rehearsed on the long flight from Sydney no longer seemed so pat, and he drew a deep breath as he struggled to find the right way to speak the words which were so important to any future they might have together. 'Maisy—'

'How's Samuel?' she asked softly, unable to hold the question in any longer.

Her tender acknowledgement of his son meant more to him than the world. 'He's beautiful. Absolutely beautiful—'

'And Re-becca?' She faltered with this question but, after all, she was only flesh and blood.

'She's. . .well. Exhausted, of course.'

'Of course,' Maisy echoed politely.

'She's planning to bring him to England just as soon as she has recovered from the birth.'

'Oh.'

'And I'm planning to live here too.'

She wanted to hurl herself into his arms and cover his face with kisses, but this was much too important a moment to cloud with passion. 'And?'

'I want you to be in full command of all the facts. It worries me that you might think I'm declaring my love for you because I'll need all the help I can get with Samuel.'

'But if that were the case then you'd stay with Rebecca, wouldn't you?' she argued logically. 'That would be infinitely more sensible. Particularly if she loves you?'

The question hung like thunder in the air. He searched carefully for the right words. 'Coming to England was the very best thing I could have done—

apart from meeting you. The separation gave Rebecca time to work a few things out, and she has realised that we had no foundation for true love. That love has to be mutual or it cannot exist. She is an attractive and intelligent woman; she'll find someone else—of that I am certain.'

'Someone who will be a father to your son?' she said deliberately, knowing that he had to face up to facts, however unpalatable they might be.

The pain which crossed his face was profound but fleeting. 'That, too,' he agreed. 'Which is why I need him to know *me*.' His green eyes glittered. 'And I need to know something else. Do you love *me*, Jackson?'

'You know I do,' she answered simply, and his smile was heartbreakingly brilliant.

'Thank God,' he murmured, and drew her into his arms as he asked his next question so softly that Maisy had to strain her ears to hear. 'And do you think you could learn to love Samuel too?'

Maisy rested her head against his chest and closed her eyes as she realised that sometimes dreams really could come true. 'Samuel is part of *you*, Matthew,' she whispered, 'and, as such, I love him already.'

'Oh, sweetheart,' he sighed against her hair. 'I know that I come with a lot of emotional baggage—'

'But who doesn't, Matthew?' asked Maisy softly. 'Who doesn't?'

He shook his dark head. 'My situation is slightly different—I come with a ready-made family! And

you may think it prudent for us not to do anything
or see one another—at least, not until things have
calmed down a little and I've sorted out some kind
of routine with Samuel. In six months' time—'

'Six *months*?' she interrupted with disbelief. 'Do
you really think I'm going to wait for another six
months when I've waited for you all my life,
Matthew Gallagher?' And she put her arms around
his neck, slowly raised her face to his and
kissed him.

It was an amazing kiss—Maisy had never before
experienced anything quite like it. She had no idea
you could kiss for so long without coming up for
air, or that kissing should so quickly provoke the
most overwhelming desire to have him make mad,
passionate love to her.

Her hands burrowed beneath his sweater as he
held her soft, buttery curls between his palms.

'Maisy—' he gasped as he dragged his mouth
away from hers with an effort, and he looked positively shaken. 'Sweet, beautiful Maisy. I want to
marry you.'

She heard the ardour which distorted the words
she had never thought he would say, and knew then
that she could not possibly marry him under false
pretences. She drew a deep, shuddering breath.
'Matthew, I've got something I need to tell you,
too—'

'Later,' he growled, as his fingers began to
unhook the buttons of her pyjama jacket.

Feeling dangerously compliant, Maisy wriggled
as far away from him as she could to the opposite

end of the sofa, wondering just how she was going to tell him and then deciding that there was no easy way.

'I'm frigid,' she said baldly.

He smiled.

'Did you hear what I said?' she demanded querulously. 'I'm *frigid*!'

His green eyes glittered. 'Says who?'

'Says Giles—and he's had hundreds of lovers so he should know!'

He swore softly, then stood up and held his hand out towards her. 'Come on,' he murmured.

'Where?'

'To bed.'

'Matthew, I *can't*.'

'You don't have to do anything,' he soothed her with a glint in his eye as he led her into the bedroom. 'Anything you don't want to do, that is.'

'But I feel like a sacrificial lamb!' she protested as some of the rigid fear began to seep away.

'Then maybe I'll cover you with mint sauce and lick it all off—'

'Matthew!'

'What?' he enquired innocently as he pulled her down onto the bed beside him. He cradled her in his arms and began to stroke her.

'Oh, Matthew,' she sighed.

'Oh, Maisy,' he smiled back.

The clock struck eleven in the darkened room where the only other sound was of breathing which had eventually slowed down to something approaching normality.

'Well?'

'Well, what? I suppose you're feeling very pleased with yourself, Matthew Gallagher!'

'Mmm. Aren't you?'

Maisy blushed. 'It was—'

'Shh. I know what it was, sweetheart—I was there too, remember?'

Their eyes met.

'Is it always like that?' she asked hesitantly.

He considered the question carefully. 'Well, the orgasm bit is mainly a question of doing the right things at the right time, but it's never been as sensational as that for me before.' His eyes crinkled with delight at the corners. 'But, then, I've never been in love before.' He stroked a silken curl away from her cheek.

'I made a mistake with Giles,' admitted Maisy, wincing as she thought of just how close she had come to marrying him.

'Giles was the one who made a mistake, sweetheart. To have treated you so badly. To have accused you of being unresponsive—a ploy commonly used by men who have an inability to give a woman pleasure.'

Maisy yawned and stretched her arms luxuriously as Giles faded from her mind for ever. 'It'll be the New Year in one hour. Jamie and Sarah are having a party—do you want to go?'

He shook his head. 'I don't want to move from this spot so why don't we have our own celebration here?' he suggested, a hungry glint illuminating his eyes.

She snuggled up to him with contentment. 'I can't think of a nicer way to see the New Year in!'

He caught sight of an open textbook on the locker. 'And how's the research going?' he asked.

'Fine,' she nodded. 'I love it. I think I've found my niche in medicine. Oh, and Nicolette's pregnant!' she announced with a grin.

'That was quick.' He frowned. 'I know I referred her—'

'She had one consultation. Just one. Her tests were all normal. Her periods were OK—and suddenly she's pregnant!'

He smiled. 'That's the way of these things. Twenty-eight per cent of women with unexplained infertility will conceive after one consultation—'

'Why?'

'No one knows, exactly—there are many complex psychological and physiological factors governing fertility. I'm delighted. Now. . .' he leaned over onto one elbow and subjected her to a piercing stare '. . .we just need to get your dysmenorrhoea sorted out and everything in the garden will be lovely!'

'Matthew!' she blushed. 'How on earth could you know something like that?'

'My job is to observe women,' he answered wryly. 'And I happened to be observing the woman I love with extra scrutiny. So when I saw you white-faced and trying not to clutch at your tummy, while taking painkillers like there was no tomorrow, I resolved to do something about it when I came back. I could hardly leave you with my parting words about dysmenorrhoea ringing in your ears!'

Something had made her puzzled. 'But you might not have come back, surely?' she objected. 'If Rebecca had wanted to stay in Australia.'

He lifted her chin with his hand so that their eyes collided in a dazzling gaze of love. 'Of course I had to come back,' he said simply. 'For you. And if Rebecca *had* wanted Samuel to be brought up in Australia then I would have done everything in my power to convince you that you could be very happy living *there*.'

'I could be happy anywhere,' she said quietly, 'just as long as you were with me.'

'I love you, Maisy,' he murmured as he lowered his mouth to hers. 'More than words can ever say.'

'Thank heavens you've stopped calling me Jackson,' she observed drily once the kiss had ended. 'I hated it.'

His mouth quirked into a reluctant and rueful line. 'Do you think I didn't know that? Did you think it had escaped my noticed that you gritted your teeth with rage every time I said it?'

'It made me feel less of a woman,' she admitted at last.

'Why else do you think I persisted, sweetheart?' he quizzed softly. '*I* needed to regard you as less of a woman because I knew, deep down, that you were the one woman I couldn't resist. And I couldn't possibly work with someone I kept having X-rated fantasies about, now could I?'

'And now?' she queried demurely. 'Do you think you could work with me now?'

'Let's fulful a few of those fantasies first,' he growled wickedly as he began to stroke the milky satin of her skin, 'and then we'll readdress the question.'

Sarah Brennan tried to telephone her sister just before midnight to persuade her to join the party, but there was no reply.

'That's funny,' she remarked to her husband as she heard the phone ring and ring. 'I'm sure she said she wasn't going out.'

Jamie smiled. He had seen his Australian counterpart getting out of a taxi earlier, but he had no intention of telling his wife until the morning! 'Perhaps she's fallen asleep,' he suggested innocently.

'Perhaps,' said Sarah doubtfully.

In Maisy's narrow bed she and Matthew heard telephone bells and church bells, but paid them no notice whatsoever as they saw the New Year in— in a way which neither of them would ever forget.

MILLS & BOON®

Medical Romance™

Dear Santa,

Please make this a special Christmas for us.
This Christmas we would like...

A VERY SPECIAL NEED by Caroline Anderson
'Daddy do you think you'll ever find another mummy
for me? I think I'd like to have a mummy,' Alice asked.

A HEALING SEASON by Jessica Matthews
Libby's children loved having Dr Caldwell around at
Christmas, but then it wasn't just the children who
liked him.

MERRY CHRISTMAS, DOCTOR DEAR by Elisabeth Scott
Colin told his Uncle Matt that you couldn't always be
sure what you got for Christmas, you just had to wait
and see, but they felt sure that this Christmas would be
worth waiting for.

A FATHER FOR CHRISTMAS by Meredith Webber
Richard tries hard to put his feelings for Margaret's
children down to a lack of sleep, but he isn't fooling
anybody, not least of all himself!

Christmas is for kids

...a family.
Thank you very much
The Children

Four books written by four authors from around
the world with one wish for Christmas.

FREE!

FOUR FREE
specially selected
Medical Romance™ novels
PLUS a FREE Mystery Gift
when you return this page...

Return this coupon and we'll send you 4 Medical Romance novels and a mystery gift absolutely FREE! We'll even pay the postage and packing for you.

We're making you this offer to introduce you to the benefits of the Reader Service™– FREE home delivery of brand-new Medical Romance novels, at least a month before they are available in the shops, FREE gifts and a monthly Newsletter packed with information, competitions, author profiles and lots more...

Accepting these FREE books and gift places you under no obligation to buy, you may cancel at any time, even after receiving just your free shipment. Simply complete the coupon below and send it to:

MILLS & BOON READER SERVICE, FREEPOST, CROYDON, SURREY, CR9 3WZ.

READERS IN EIRE PLEASE SEND COUPON TO PO BOX 4546, DUBLIN 24

NO STAMP NEEDED

Yes, please send me 4 free Medical Romance novels and a mystery gift. I understand that unless you hear from me, I will receive 4 superb new titles every month for just £2.20* each, postage and packing free. I am under no obligation to purchase any books and I may cancel or suspend my subscription at any time, but the free books and gift will be mine to keep in any case. (I am over 18 years of age)

M7YE

Ms/Mrs/Miss/Mr_____
BLOCK CAPS PLEASE

Address_____

_____

_____ Postcode _____

LaVyrle
SPENCER

✳

The Hellion

Two Hearts...Worlds Apart

As teenagers they had shared a wild and reckless love—and had been forced to pay the highest price. Now, three broken marriages later, Tommy Lee Gentry has come knocking on Rachel Hollis' door, begging to be given another another chance.

"LaVyrle Spencer has written a truly special story...The Hellion is nostalgic and captures the feelings of love lost and years wasted...SUPERB!"

—Chicago Sun Times

Jennifer
BLAKE

GARDEN
of
SCANDAL

She wants her life back...

Branded a murderer, Laurel Bancroft has
been a recluse for years. Now she wants her
life back--but someone in her past will do
anything to ensure the truth stays buried.

*"Blake's style is as steamy as a still July
night...as overwhelmingly hot as Cajun spice."*
— Chicago Tribune

GET TO KNOW

THE BEST OF ENEMIES

the latest blockbuster from TAYLOR SMITH

Who would you trust with your life? Think again.

Linked to a terrorist bombing, a young student goes missing. One woman believes in the girl's innocence and is determined to find her before she is silenced. Leya Nash has to decide—quickly—who to trust. The wrong choice could be fatal.

Valid only in the UK & Ireland against purchases made in retail outlets and not in conjunction with any Reader Service or other offer.